Cindy Lou leaned forward pinkly, blinked her five-pointed eyes, and allowed the pink negligee to slip from her bosom to reveal the pink outlines of pink nipples under the extremely thin pink material of her shortie nightie.

"Our husbands don't score, Steve. That's our problem. My problem! We simply can't wait any longer for them. We need satisfaction now! Now!" Cindy Lou bent towards me panting, lips moist, generous breasts heaving, thighs flushed. "What should we do, Steve?" Her hand burned on my thigh. "What should *I* do?"

"I don't really think—"

"Help me, Steve!" Cindy Lou put her arms around me, pressed her soft breasts against my chest, and leaned back with her eyes half-closed and her pink lips parted and waiting to be kissed. "Help me!"

"Listen." I tried to resist. "The first game is just around the corner. With Terry quarterbacking, the team's bound to score. Just be patient, and your husband—"

"I can't be patient." There were tears in her eyes. "I need satisfaction. I need it now." She unzipped my fly and slipped to her knees in front of me. "I'm desperate!"

THE GUNN SERIES BY JORY SHERMAN

THE MAN FROM O.R.G.Y.

THE TIGHT END
TED MARK

ZEBRA BOOKS

KENSINGTON PUBLISHING CORP.

ZEBRA BOOKS

are published by

KENSINGTON PUBLISHING CORP.
475 Park Avenue South
New York, N.Y. 10016

Printed in the United States of America

AUTHOR'S NOTE

There is no such team in either professional football conference as the Whittier Stonewalls. While the Pittsburgh Steelers and the Philadelphia Eagles are of course actual and renowned professional football teams, and the names of real players on both teams are mentioned in this work, this is to certify that no such games as those described herein actually took place and the participation of those mentioned by their real names is completely a matter of the author's imagination. The games described are meant solely as entertainment and in no way to reflect on the considerable abilities of those Steelers and Eagles mentioned by name. It is the author's hope that all those involved in professional football will get some of the enjoyment back through reading this book that the author has received over the years as a spectator of the sport.

—Ted Mark

CHAPTER ONE

Ahhhh! Superbowl Sunday!

At the foot of the bed the color TV was on, the rabbit-ears finely tuned. I'd cracked open the six-pack and the first beer was already flowing down my gullet. On the screen the players stood at attention as the national anthem was sung. Beside me, under the sheets, Stephanie Greenwillow squeezed my penis.

The beer cooled my belly. Stephanie warmed my erection in her hands. Oakland kicked off. Superbowl XV was under way. God bless America!

All was right with my world.

Almost . . .

"Why do they all jump on that one man with the ball so brutally?" Stephanie inquired indignantly.

"It's their job to stop him."

"But they're so big!"

"They're defensive linemen. They're supposed to be big."

"They're doing it again! It's not fair! He's already on the ground and they're piling on top of him!"

"Stephanie! Don't sit up like that! You're blocking the screen!"

"But look! That's vicious! Look what they're doing!"

"How can I look if you're blocking the screen?"

"I don't care! It's sheer brutality! It's a clear illustration of football as metaphor for man's inhumanity to man, wars, exploitation, inhumane—"

"Interception! Interception!" I couldn't tell whether it was Engberg or Olsen announcing the pick-off from the set behind Stephanie. "Martin gets back to the Eagles' thirty from the forty-six and he's brought down there."

"Stephanie," I begged. "Get out of the way so I can see the instant replay."

"The what?"

"The instant replay."

"What's that?"

I explained.

"You mean they show the same thing over again? What's the point?"

"The point is that if a naked woman pops up in front of the screen so you miss the play the first time, you get a second shot at seeing it."

"My goodness! They do think of everything, don't they?"

"Lie down, Stephanie!" Too late! The replay was over. I'd missed it.

"Don't be grumpy." Stephanie's red hair fanned out over my face, tickling my cheeks as she

8

kissed me. Her large, round, naked breasts, the red nipples stiff, pressed against my bare chest. The swollen purple lips of her vagina nipped at my aroused phallus.

It worked. My grumpiness subsided. It's hard to stay mad when a young woman like Stephanie lays out the feast of her voluptuous body for you.

I licked her nipples. She bit my ear. I stroked her clitoris. She fondled my balls. I moaned. She moaned. And then—

"TOUCHDOWN! TOUCHDOWN!" The crowd was roaring. "Branch has the scoring pass and Oakland's on the board!"

"Damn!" I shot up in the bed, almost shoving Stephanie to the floor. "Godammit to hell!"

"What's the matter?"

"The matter? The matter? I bet Philly and I gave three! That's the matter! And I didn't even get to see the goddam touchdown!"

"You mean you'd rather watch these Neander-thals pulverize each other than—than—" Stephanie was sitting up again, blocking the TV set, hands indignantly on hips.

"Christ! Now I missed the conversion!"

It was my own fault. I'd been listening to Stephanie Greenwillow putting down football since the pre-season games back in early September. Stephanie was a dedicated feminist, author of *The Moving Needle*, a definitive work on rape and seduction from the victim's point of view. Her anti-pathy to gridiron mayhem came with the territory. I should have known better that night a week before the Superbowl than to challenge her attitude.

"You run off at the mouth about 'macho' and 'violence' and 'brutality' and 'the battered wife syndrome' and 'frontier mentality' and all sorts of other disconnected—not to say remote—items, and you lump them all in with football, and the truth is you don't really know the first goddam thing about the game!" I'd accused her. "Why, I'll bet you've never even seen a pro football game."

"I've never seen a war either. I don't have to see one to know I'm opposed to it."

"Football isn't war."

"It's all part of the same sick *manly* syndrome."

"Bull! There's no connection! Football isn't just physical. It's intellectual and esthetic too. It can be like a game of chess. A well executed play can be like a perfectly choreographed ballet."

Yeah, I know. It was a bit much. But what do you expect? She had me on the defensive.

"It's a primary symptom of what's wrong with our society!"

"There you go again! You're just parroting the liberated woman's party line. At least watch a game, so you know what you're talking about."

She thought about it a minute. "All right," she decided grudgingly. "I'll watch a game with you next Sunday."

"Next Sunday is Superbowl Sunday."

"Isn't that all right?"

"Oh, sure. Sure."

Superbowl Sunday! My luck!

So here we were. The game was only a smidgeon

10

over six minutes old, and I'd already missed the first interception, the first touchdown, and the first conversion. I wondered if feminists feel as strongly about murder as they do about rape.

Stephanie was sulking. "Do you think it would be all right if I had a beer?" she asked with petulant sarcasm. "Or would that be too much of a distraction?"

"Sure, baby. Have a beer." My bitterness gave way to remorse. I'm a sucker for guilt trips, and after all, she was my guest. Her watching the game with me was my own doing. "Let's be friends." I kissed the little pulse at the base of her neck.

I didn't have to see the red light flashing or hear the bells jangling to know I'd hit right on target. The sensitivity of that pulse was one of the first things I'd learned about Stephanie when we'd started sleeping together on a steady basis about a month before the start of the gridiron season. Kissing her there was key to fulfilling all of the erotic fantasies her body aroused in me.

It's the kind of body that's sometimes described as Amazonian, or Junoesque. Stephanie being a leading feminist, such descriptions, I suppose, are inevitable. But there is an implication in them of unyielding flesh which is very far from the reality of Stephanie.

She may be tall and hold herself tall, but she is also very soft and womanly. Her breasts are large and creamy and welcoming as fleece. Her long legs are sleek and shapely. Water jugs might be slung easily from her hips, and when they are in motion their rhythm is the raw stuff from which erections

11

are erected. Her behind is high and plump, compact and springy. Lascivious traps lurk deep in her jade-green eyes and when she discards her inhibitions in bed, her mane of red hair swirls about like a demanding whirlpool sucking one deeper and deeper into the tempestuous depths of her libido.

Phew! But it's true, all true!

Now my kissing of the pulse at the base of her neck unlocked that libido. She dug her nails into my back and spread her thighs and moaned and bounced on her volatile bottom. "Steve!" She kissed me urgently, her tongue deep in my mouth. "Ahh! . . . I'm . . . so . . . hot!"

My cock, flat up against my naked belly and prodding, told me it was mutual. Lying atop her, I rested my chest on the pillow of her breasts. Her long, excited, blood-red nipples burned into my flesh. I reached down and my fingers tangled in the silky hair over her Mound of Venus. I probed and found her honey hot and flowing. I played with her clitty and she sank her teeth into the muscle of my shoulder. "Don't tease me," she panted. And her ass burned and writhed under my squeezing, stroking hand. "Please! Please!"

I shifted position. I raised her legs over my arms and placed them on my shoulders, placed them high so that her thighs, their muscles straining and the insides shiny with a mixture of syrup and perspiration, pressed against my upper chest. This bent her long body double and raised her pussy and spread it wide. Sopping as it was, it was also deliciously tight and thrillingly ridged. I eased my cock inside her, savoring the rippling sensation.

And then I began to pump with short, hard, deep, punishing strokes.

Stephanie began beating a tattoo on my shoulders with her fists. "Fuck!" she snarled, half crying. "Fuck!" And she slammed her pussy against me in a manner that kept my hot balls swinging, a manner that insisted that she was fucking me every bit as much as I was fucking her.

We went at it for a long time. Sometimes we pumped. Sometimes we screwed. Sometimes we teased and sometimes we punished. We aroused and we held off and then we aroused each other again. And we made verbal demands on each other as we humped:

"Squeeze my balls as I come down inside you!"

"Suck my nipples hard!"

"Ride up and down on it!"

"Play with my ass!"

"Squeeze tighter! Tighter!"

"Harder! Faster! Harder! Faster!"

"I'm gonna fuck the ass off you, Stephanie!"

"Yes! Yes! Yes! ... Oh! I'm going to come! ... I can feel it! ... Your cock is—! Ooh! ... I'm going to come!"

And just then—

"Jaworski to Rodney Parker, and it's touchdown Eagles!"

My head shot up and turned as if my neck was double-jointed. Hell, I was betting Philly. Shit! I was just in time to hear the play called back. Illegal motion!

"What's that? What did you say?" Stephanie panted.

13

"Illegal motion!"

"What's that?"

"Something like this!" I told her, slamming my cock so high up her cunt that I momentarily breached the mouth of her womb.

"Oh, darling!" She began playing her own version of Ravel's *Bolero* with her quim.

I danced to her tune. Once again we writhed in sync, building to orgasm. Once again we took our time, savoring, teasing, fucking intimately, deep and hard. Once again we reached the point where Stephanie announced "I'm going to come!" And once again—

The crowd roared. Both announcers were shouting at once. By the time I managed to crane my neck around again, it was over. King had taken a pass from Plunkett and gone eighty yards for the Raiders' second touchdown.

"What is it? What happened?" Stephanie, still writhing, noticed that I wasn't writhing back.

"Touchdown."

"What? What did you say?"

"Touchdown. A record-breaker. The longest play in Superbowl history."

"The longest—" Suddenly Stephanie's foot drew back and shot forward into my face. Her next kick went right between the goalposts to score a devastating blow to my testicles. And then she was out from under me and storming across the room. "I don't believe you!" she was screaming. "I just don't believe you!"

"Listen." I tried to explain. "Try to understand. I took the Eagles and gave three points. Sentiment.

Next to New York, the nicest people live in Philly.''
The pain in my balls was making me babble.
"What I mean, this is real tragedy. A TD called
back. And now a fluke eighty yard run!"

"You listen to yourself! Just listen to yourself!
There I am about to come and you—! Ooh! And
now you stand here trying to tell me—! Ooh! I
don't believe you! Ooh! I just don't believe you!
Can this be Steve Victor behaving this way? Can
this be Steve Victor, the reknowned man from
O.R.G.Y.?"

"Come on now, Stephanie! What does that have
to do—?"

"Steve Victor, the illustrious sex expert!" she
jeered."The fair haired boy of the sex research
grant circuit! The sex-master who'd rather get his
rocks off watching barbarians clash over a pig's
bladder than satisfy a woman! Yes, Steve Victor,
whom they mention in the same breath with Kinsey
and Masters and Johnson and Comfort, but whose
real heroes are bone-breaking behemoths in human
form. The Man from O.R.G.Y. indeed!"

"O.R.G.Y.," I reminded her frostily, "is not
meant to indicate my status. It stands for
'Organization for the Rational Guidance of
Youth'."

"And is this what you call rational guidance?
Make touchdowns, not love!"

"You're beautiful when you're angry." I tried to
lighten the hostility with a joke.

It was a mistake. Stephanie's sense of humor was
on vacation. She took the remark as an insult.
"Don't you dare condescend to me!" And she

15

began scrambling into her clothes.

It took the rest of the first half to convince her to stay. I missed the Eagles' field goal early in the second quarter. I didn't see the Oakland attempt which failed. Neither did I view the second attempt by Philly in the closing minutes, nor the spectacular move by Ted Hendricks which blocked it.

Stephanie and I spent halftime getting it on again. We got into it so deeply that I didn't even miss a stroke at the beginning of the second half when Branch wrestled Plunkett's pass away from Young in the end zone to put the Raiders ahead twenty-one to three. Nor did I allow Bahr's subsequent field goal to distract me. Hell, at twenty-four to three, I figured my bet was down the drain anyway. I put Philly-spot-three out of my mind and humped in keeping with my reputation as Steve Victor, the one-and-only Man from O.R.G.Y. The best rational guidance one can supply youth, after all, is to set an example.

"Ooh!" Stephanie was appreciative. "Ahh! . . . There! Stick it there! That's right! . . . Now there! Harder! . . . Ahh! Ahh! Ahh!" Her ass burned red hot to my balls bouncing off it.

The fourth quarter began with a grinding corkscrew motion that had the two of us twisting like tortured tops. Jaworski connected with Keith Krepfle and the Eagles had their first TD. "Don't!" Stephanie moaned when I showed signs of interest in this development. Obediently I kept screwing while I listened for confirmation of the extra point. *Who do I know who might be getting*

16

this on video cassette? I wondered to myself as I pounded away at the panting, moaning, writhing redhead.

"Now, Steve! I'm there again! I'm going to come! I'm—"

Bahr kicked a thirty-five yard field goal to make it twenty-seven to ten and my telephone rang.

"Don't stop!" Stephanie begged as I answered it.

"Hello." I didn't stop.

"Hello, is this Steve Victor of the Organization for the Rational Guidance of Youth?"

"I'm coming! I'm co—!"

"Yes. This is Steve Victor."

"This is Charles Putnam, Mr. Victor. Do you remember me?"

Did I remember him? Did Faust remember Mephistopheles? *Now* I stopped.

"Steve! What happened? You went all soft!" Stephanie was in tears.

"I remember you," I told Charles Putnam grimly.

"Good. Then I'll come directly to the point. I have need of your services, Mr. Victor."

Collection Day for Souls, Brother Faust! I flopped limply out of the distraught Stephanie. "Need of my services," I echoed. The words were like a warning bell reminding me of just who the devil was on the other end of my phone.

Charles Putnam, in the days when I'd had dealings with him, was the top shadow executive of the United States government. His niche was

17

somewhere in the cracks between the spheres of diplomacy and espionage. Here, snugly hooked into the State Department and the CIA, although acknowledged by neither, Putnam influenced such decisions as the Bay of Pigs, the assassination attempts on Castro, the establishment of a series of puppet regimes in Vietnam, the toppling of Allende in Chile, the training of secret police for the Shah of Iran, the extrication of the Pahlevi booty when the Ayatollah came frothing to power, and many others less well known. Presidents from Eisenhower through Carter had been guided by his judgments in their continuation of U.S. foreign policy. And yet, according to each of them in turn, Charles Putnam did not exist.

His colorless persona was undisturbed by grey hair, a grey face, and an addiction to custom-made grey flannel suits which followed fashion in the width of their lapels, but otherwise were indistinguishable one from the other. The epitome of the laid-back policy setter, he was so adept at fading into the background as to have all but mastered the art of invisibility. The compleat patriot, the revelation of error in no way diminished his dedication. If the wrong cables were sometimes sent and the wrong armies sometimes moved (or the right armies in the wrong direction), Charles Putnam nevertheless pursued his course unquestioningly and without deviation, secure in his faith that despite minor misjudgments the rightness of *Our Cause* must ultimately prevail. His patriotic fervor was both dynamic and inspirational. So much so, indeed, that I had myself responded to it on more than one occasion in the past.

Need of my services... "Espionage?" Those past experiences phrased the question I now spoke into the telephone.

"Oh, no, Mr. Victor. I'm retired from government service," Putnam informed me.

On the TV screen the game was winding down. In the bed beside me, Stephanie was glaring at me and playing with herself. "If not spying, then what?" I asked.

"I can only answer that, Mr. Victor, by asking you a question." I could visualize his thin lips pursing. "What is the major focus of America today?"

I glanced at the TV set. The camera panned over the filled bleachers. Prime time. Sunday night. Millions watching. "The Superbowl," I replied.

"Quite right." Putnam agreed. "Football. That is the main concern of America today. The gridiron is a microcosm of our nation—its raw energy, its spirit of cooperation, its smooth performance, its aspirations and goals. Indeed, American ideals are both formulated and expressed on the gridiron."

Jesus! I glanced at Stephanie. Maybe she was right about football after all.

"What are you getting at, Mr. Putnam? Just what is it that you want from me?"

"Some associates of mine have asked me to retain your services as an expert in the field of sexuality. The assignment has to do with football."

"I'm not interested. I don't like working for you or your 'associates', Mr. Putnam. In the past, no

19

matter how it started out, it always ended up with somebody shooting at me. I don't like being shot at, Mr. Putnam."

"This assignment isn't like that, Mr. Victor. There is no danger."

"Ha!" I snorted disbelievingly. "The answer is still no."

"Would a great deal of money influence you to change your mind, Mr. Victor?"

I would not put a .45 slug into my mother for a great deal of money. I would not perpetrate atrocities against little children. I would not commit vivisection on cocker spaniel puppies. I would not vote for Ed Koch. Such are the principles I would not violate for a great deal of money. There may be a few others, but Putnam's proposition did not seem to be among them.

"How much money is a great deal?" I inquired cautiously.

Putnam mentioned a figure.

"That, " I granted, "is a great deal of money."

"I thought that you would think so, Mr. Victor. Stephanie's tongue was licking one of her elongated red nipples. Two fingers of her hand were plunging in and out between her straining thighs. Her gasps were audible. Her eyes were slowly crossing.

"What do I have to do for it?" I asked Putnam.

"Are you familiar with the plight of the Whittier Stonewalls, Mr. Victor?"

"Sure. The Walls are the joke team of professional football. They just ended in the sub-basement for the second season in a row. Any third

20

grade Little League team could take 'em without eating their Wheaties. But why would they interest you and your associates?"

"Sentiment."

I thought about that. "Bullshit!" I decided.

"Suppose I told you that my associates own a controlling interest in the Whittier Stonewalls, Mr. Victor?"

"Now that kind of sentiment I understand. But how do you come to be associated with people with such lousy business judgment, Mr. Putnam?"

"We provided the financial backing to enfranchise and run the team. No matter what you may think, it was and is pure altruism. We are paying tribute to the most famous bench-warmer in Whittier College football history. Surely I need not identify this statesman by name, Mr. Victor."

"Nope. But why would you want to honor a 'statesman' whose most famous public utterance is 'I am not a thief'?"

"Compassion, Mr. Victor. Our sole motivation has been compassion towards one who once held, after all, the highest office in our land."

"Which he left, in a manner of speaking, one jump ahead of the bank examiners."

"Nevertheless, his fall moved us deeply." Putnam ignored my cynicism. "When he held power, he had been sensitive to my associates' interests, and so there was—and is—an obligation to cushion his fall from grace. Knowing how fondly he looked back on his college football days, aware of his ongoing interest in the sport, what better tribute to occupy his mind than a professional football team based in Whittier."

"Why Whittier? Why not the San Clemente Plumbers, or even the Washington Watergates?"

"Ooh!" Stephanie writhed. Her hand was a fist now, buried in the sleek red pubic curls. "Ooh!"

Putnam disregarded my alternatives. "Our tribute, however, has backfired. The Stonewalls, as you pointed out, are a professional football joke. In the two years of their existence, they are zero for thirty-six. That zero, by the way, does not only stand for games won. It also is the number of points they have scored to date. This record has pushed the statesman they were to honor into a deep and desolate depression worse than any he has ever experienced. He walks the streets of your city muttering bitterly to himself about six crises, a catastrophe, and now this!"

"In New York nobody will pay attention. They'll think he's just another subway rider."

"This is not a time for levity, Mr. Victor. It is affecting his health. My associates are concerned. Something must be done about the Stonewalls!"

"How about a new team?"

"Exactly, Mr. Victor. And where would you start?"

"Quarterback, I guess. You had eight last season and not one of them ever completed a pass. Two of them broke the all-time league record for being sacked."

"Right, Mr. Victor. Now how would you go about getting a competent quarterback?"

Pondering the question, I glanced at Stephanie. Humankind, the anthropologists used to say, is distinguished from animals by the opposing thumb. It is this which grants human beings the dexterity to evolve. At the moment, Stephanie was evolving by using one opposing thumb to hold wide the swollen purple lips of her pussy in order to strum her protruding, rigid red clitoris with her other opposing thumb. The smile on her lips was both anguished and ecstatic.

"Draft picks." I answered Putnam's question.

"Four of this year's Whittier quarterbacks were first round draft picks."

"You're supposed to scout them first."

"We did scout them. And we just discharged the scouts and hired new ones. Indeed, one of those hired is a friend of yours, Mr. Victor, a former professional football defensive tackle known as 'Rhino' Dubrowski. Christian name, Elmer."

"How did you know that Rhino is a friend of mine?"

"More than a friend, surely, Mr. Victor. He was a Marine serving in Vietnam when you were there on assignment for me just before the final excrement hit the helicopter blades. He saved your life as Saigon was falling. You are eternally grateful to him. It's our business to know these things, Mr. Victor."

"I thought you said you were retired."

"Old habits die hard." Putnam's laugh was as dry as a peanut butter sandwich in a sub-Sahara drought. "In any case, your friend Dubrowski claims to have discovered a sensational young quarterback playing sandlot football in Little Rock, Arkansas. He says that this quarterback can pass, fake and run—all to perfection. The name of the quarterback is Terry Niemath.''

Stephanie was lying on her back now, her sleek legs stretched straight up in the air at a very wide angle. The candle from the night table (I always keep a candle handy in case of sudden blackouts; with Con Ed you never know) was clutched in her hands, moving in and out of her like a piston. She was bouncing so energetically that the undersides of her breasts were slapping against her rib-cage. The nipples stuck up like miniature markers signaling quivering red lust.

"Terry as in Bradshaw?" I asked Putnam.

"That's correct."

"Namath as in Joe?"

"Not quite. It's spelled N-i-e-m-a-t-h."

"Close enough if you believe in omens."

"Mr. Dubrowski says this quarterback is as good as Terry Bradshaw and Joe Namath put together," Putnam told me.

"Well, Rhino should know. When he played pro tackle he could never lay a hand on either one of them." I watched Stephanie bouncing and groaning, moaning and bouncing. Then she was suddenly quite still, the candle buried in her quim, poised on the razor-edge of orgasm. It was disconcerting. "If the guy's that good, then what's the problem?" I forced my attention back to Putnam.

"Sex."

"Could you be more specific?"

"Unfortunately, I cannot. Your friend Mr. Dubrowski refused to go into detail. He said he wanted to consult with a sex expert and he suggested you. We were in effect faced with a choice of either discharging him or acceding to his request. Needing a quarterback so desperately, we opted for calling you, Mr. Victor.''

"And if I didn't agree to help you," I realized, "Rhino would be canned. But just what is it that you expect me to do?"

"Proceed to Little Rock immediately. See Mr. Dubrowski. Determine what the sex problem involving the quarterback is. Devise a plan for dealing with it if you can. Then come to San Francisco and report to us."

"All right," I agreed. Hell, the money was good and I really did owe it to Rhino. I exchanged a few more words with Putnam and then I hung up the phone.

"AAARRRGGGHHH!" Stephanie screamed ecstatically. "I'M COMING! I'M COMING! I'M COMING!" It sounded familiar.

"And so the final score is Raiders twenty-seven, Eagles ten," Merlin Olsen summed up. So much for my bet.

"I CAME! I CAME!"

"You might have waited for me." I was pissed.

"I might have. But I didn't. It's like my favorite feminist, Flo Kennedy, said: 'A woman without a man is like a fish without a bicycle.' ''

"Fuck you!"

"Sorry," Stephanie trilled. "Too late!"

She was right. It was too late. As with the Superbowl XV, I'd missed the climax.

CHAPTER TWO

"Anal defecation!" On the other side of the picture window of the motel bar the Monday night traffic of Little Rock, Arkansas, was light as it zinged its way towards the fun part of town. "Kidney fluid!" Rhino Dubrowski wasn't paying attention to the traffic. His mind was on his own problems. "And corruption!" he finalized, downing another in a long line of bourbons.

Rhino wasn't happy. When Rhino wasn't happy, he drank and he cursed. He drank pretty much the way everybody drinks. His cursing, however, was uniquely his own.

A former Marine, a former pro football lineman, at six-foot-six and two-hundred ninety pounds, walking away from you, Rhino looked like the back end of a steamroller. From the neck up he resembled the rhinoceros for which he had been nicknamed, except for his eyes, which were pure basset hound with an alcohol problem. The problem affected his cursing style slightly, but it didn't really change it.

"Cohabitating pain in the anus!" he mumbled, pouring another bourbon from the bottle he'd had the bartender leave at our table. Marine or not, pro tackle or not, Rhino had been brought up to watch his language, and the upbringing stuck. Four-letter Anglo-Saxon words never crossed his thick, blubbery lips. However, the impetus—the sentiment and the fury—was there for Rhino as it is for all of us when Fate sneaks in a particularly low blow. "No-good phallus-ingesting quarterback!"

The customary curses were translated in this fashion before they crossed Rhino's lips. The snarling tone with which they were delivered, however, left no doubt that they were as heartfelt as their locker-room equivalents. And, given Rhino's brawn, nobody was about to criticize the translations as being sissified.

"Why don't you tell me the problem, old buddy?" I suggested for perhaps the tenth time since I'd joined Rhino in the cocktail lounge of the Little Rock motel where I was staying.

This time he pulled himself together enough to attempt a reply. He lubricated his voice box with another slug of bourbon and then he answered. "The problem, old buddy, is that the quarterback would rather ball than play ball." The basset hound eyes filled with pain as he used the word 'ball' to designate the sex act. It was the closest I'd ever heard Rhino come to using bad language, including the time he'd saved my life in 'Nam, an incident hairy enough to inspire longshoreman lingo from

27

the tongue of a Mother Superior who'd taken vows of silence.

"So, since when are pro football players sworn to chastity?" I responded. "Hell, you know better than that, Rhino. Besides, there are some really super-beautiful women in Little Rock, from what I've seen. I don't blame the guy."

"Fecal matter!" Rhino's wide head wobbled drunkenly on his thick neck. "You're not reading the signals, Steve. I'm telling you that Terry Niemath would rather ball the players than play with the ball!"

I stared at him. He tried to stare back, but his eyeballs kept getting lost in the basset hound pouches. "This quarterback doesn't like women?" I said slowly.

Rhino made a noise like a Kikuyu spear had just been stuck in his hide. "You're beginning to catch on, old buddy. Ain't that a urinator?"

"Terry Niemath is gay?"

My friend emitted a noncommital snort, as if about to plunge into a mudhole. Instead, he toppled forward onto the table and passed out cold. The maneuver was not unlike that of a monument falling.

"Gay," I repeated to myself. "What do you know about that?"

After I put Rhino Dubrowski to bed in my room, I went back down to the bar and had another drink by myself. I had to think. I sipped the scotch slowly and did just that.

Rhino was in bad shape. The toot he was on

looked like it might be several days old. He was at that stage where the booze went down smooth as water, until the point when the brain turned out the switch.

He was my buddy. I owed him. This quarterback problem had him on the ropes. It was up to me to do something about it.

Rhino hadn't given me much to work with before he zonked out. I'd managed to pry loose some facts about quarterback Terry Niemath from him before his final fizzle, but not too many. As I thought about them now, sloshing the melting ice cube around my scotch with my middle finger, they seemed less and less helpful.

Terry Niemath was a nineteen-year-old who'd dropped out of Little Rock Central High at the age of sixteen. Terry's mother had died giving birth to Terry, who was an only child. Terry's father was an evangelical fundamentalist preacher who'd thrown Terry out of the house for giggling while singing *Drop-Kick Me, Jesus, Through the Goal Posts of Life* at the close of a prayer meeting. According to Terry, Daddy Niemath refused to join the Moral Majority because he thought Reverend Jerry Falwell was too permissive.

Since the split, Terry had gotten by with a series of odd jobs including playing bush league football with Sunday morning pickup teams. Terry had made quite a name as a quarterback around the state of Arkansas. Rhino had heard the talk and one of his first moves as a scout for the Whittier Stonewalls had been to check out Terry.

"The kid was fantastic!" he'd told me before the

bourbon took over. "Pair of hands like Fran Tarkenton. A head for calling plays like Bart Starr. Tricky as Unitas and fast as Luckman. Most fornicating one hundred thirty-nine pounds of quarterback on the hoof I ever did see! A real kidney-reliever!"

"A hundred thirty-nine pounds? Jesus, Rhino, nobody that light can play pro football!"

"This kid can! Greased lightning! Knows how to fall with the hit too."

"A hundred thirty-nine pounds know how to fall with two ninety on top? You've got to be kidding, Rhino."

But he wasn't kidding. He was dead serious. He reminded me of how little Namath had weighed in his prime. Which was true, but that was still a bundle over one-three-nine.

"You gotta see it to believe it," he told me.

"Okay. When do I meet this marvel?" I wanted to know.

"I'll take you over soon as we have one more drink. I got Terry a room at my motel to be on the safe side."

Only the one more after the one more had kept Rhino from doing that. Hell, I decided, I'd go look up this Terry Niemath by myself. Maybe we could discuss this gay problem. Maybe it wasn't a problem at all. Maybe Rhino was just over-reacting to it out of his leatherneck jock background. Still, he had implied that Terry might be making passes at his teammates off the field as well as on. At one hundred thirty-nine pounds, that could be a very big problem. It would only be a matter of time before he came on with the wrong guy and got himself hammered into the ground. Gay is one thing. Foolhardy is another. Grab-assing the wrong linebacker could be very foolhardy. Very foolhardy indeed! Yeah, I'd best look up this Terry Niemath and have a talk with him.

The Riverview Motel where Rhino and Terry Niemath were staying was a couple of rungs down the old traveling-man ladder from mine. One look at it, and I knew that Rhino's expense account must have a short leash. The overage desk clerk must have been a loser in the last Little Rock bubble gum-blowing contest. The result was tangled all through his stubble. Watching him pop one as I came through the door, I could see why. The poor sixty-odd-year-old kid hadn't quite gotten the hang of it yet.

"Try puffing in your cheeks a little instead of puffing 'em out," I suggested.

He popped another bubble all over himself and didn't deign to answer.

"Terry Niemath in?" I inquired.

"Nope."

"Know where I can find him?"

He looked at me peculiarly, dribbling stickum from the corner of his mouth. I guessed from the look that the bubble-popper had pegged Terry as gay. Probably he thought I was, too, and that was why I was looking for him. "Football stadium," he said finally, his latest bubble attempt disintegrating in a spray of saliva.

I glanced at the clock behind him. It was after

midnight. "This late at night?" I reacted. "What for?"

"Practice." He laughed and the resulting mess stopped up his nose and got in the corners of his eyes. "Football practice. All the players down there."

"Just where is the football stadium?" I backed away from his struggles.

He told me. I left. Behind me, the oldster was trying to rub the gum out of his cheeks with cleaning fluid.

Ten minutes later I pulled my rented car up in the parking lot behind the football stadium and doused the lights. There were half a dozen other cars already parked there. One of the exit doors from the stadium was flapping open in the wind. I crossed over to it and went inside.

It was dark. I followed the ramp by feel and emerged in the grandstand at about the fifty-yard line. Here, it was unexpectedly bright. I glanced up at the sky. There was a moon there, and some stars, but that accounted for only part of the brightness. I looked behind me. Yeah. One bank of spotlights had been turned on to illuminate a section of the field in front of the goalposts to my right.

As I started following the aisle through the grandstand to get closer to the pool of light, there was a sudden commotion from across the field. A stream of beefy flesh was pouring out of one of the team dressing rooms. I blinked and looked again.

They sure looked like football players all right. Lots of muscle, lots of heft, lots of concentration, lots of aggressiveness. They were dressed like football players too—after a fashion. What I mean is that almost all of them were wearing helmets, some were wearing jerseys, a few were wearing shoulder pads, chest protectors, shin guards, and/or cleats. Not one, however, was wearing uniform pants, any kind of underpants, or even a jock strap. Bulling and snarling their way onto the field, they looked like so many hot dog vendors waving their weenies in the wind.

Most of them were also waving moonshine jugs or beer bottles. The mild wind mixed the scent of burning pot with the magnolia fragrance of the chill Arkansas air. Their shouts of uninhibited obscenities crackled through the night.

What the hell? The quarterback, evidently, wasn't the only one on the team who was gay. Judging from the testicle-swinging game of leapfrog going on downfield, this team might have been recruited by Truman Capote as a muscular memorial to Mae West. And they sure were brawny, all right. There was nothing at all effete about these guys. There must have been a built-in gym in the closet out of which they'd come. Their scrimmages must really be a gas!

You shouldn't leap to conclusions. When I refocused my eyes a moment later, I realized that. What I saw, stretched out seductively between the goal posts, was a sight which both explained the nudity and high spirits of the guys on the field and, at the same time, shattered the gay mold into which I'd cast them.

What I saw was a naked blonde who was to your average selection of naked blondes what the Mona

Lisa is to a kindergarten display of finger paintings!

Some hunk of gridiron equipment! She was tall and voluptuous with firm, healthy, glowing flesh. In that very first moment of looking at her, I realized how much she resembled Stephanie Greenwillow.

Stephanie was a redhead, of course, and this girl had blonde hair which she wore shorter than quite a few guys I knew. Still, her long, limber, curvaceous body was remarkably like Stephanie's and, while her face had more of an adolescent openness, the high cheekbones, the full sensual lips, and the tilted chin were all quite similar. Later, when I drew closer, I would see that her eyes were a different color—blue, where Stephanie's were green—and her nose, a different shape—snub, where Stephanie's was classically Grecian.

Now, however, like the turned on football players, I was focusing on her body, and what she was doing with it. An end zone Circe, she was on her knees and swaying so that all of her best points might be appreciated. On the whole it was a very generous body, and the whole was made up of some very generous parts.

Her legs, even bent at the knees and with her weight resting on them, were sleek and slender. The muscles of her thighs stood out gracefully without bulging. Her hips were well-padded, but in no way heavy. Her bottom—ah, her bottom—!

It was a work of art, pure and simple! The cheeks were high and glowing and provocative as if molded by some sassy erotic sculptor. The cleft between them was a deep, pink valley promising wild, warm wigglings. Yeah, her ass proclaimed itself boldly, its movements announcing even now that it knew no inhibitions.

She was long-waisted, quite slim from the tapering of her upper torso to the flare of her hips. Her belly was flat, the skin covering it tight and tan. She was a girl who did her exercises and took her sun *au naturel*. Her deep navel was as sensual as an Egyptian dancer in motion.

The provocative swaying brought her breasts into prominence. The spotlights highlighted their golden tan and bright red berry nipples. They were large, like Stephanie's, missile-shaped and carried high, with their delicious-looking tips pointing skyward.

A handful to fill the shovel-paws of any overdeveloped pass-receiver! Or a mouthful for a guy like me who was weaned too early!

Now she shifted position. She was on her heels, squatting, rocking back and forth. Her thighs were wide apart, her knees pointing outward in opposite directions. This revealed her pussy completely.

It was framed by a triangle of very light-colored, very curly blonde hair. The mound this covered was quite pronounced—very high, very plump. It was cleft deep and opened wide to reveal inflamed purple lips and the bright red meatiness of female flesh engorged with lust. A deep, tight tunnel receded from this flesh. Squinting, as I came directly opposite her in the grandstand now, I could see that the entrance to the tunnel was silvery-moist and pulsating.

Suddenly she loosed a loud rebel yell. Then she

spoke in a voice that was quite calm and soft by contrast, but quite insistent, as well. "Y'all gonna keep on hootin' an' hollerin' there whilst I set here on my bare, burnin' butt a-waitin' an' a-wantin'?" She tossed her short blonde curls demandingly.

"Yes, Ma'am!" A hefty fullback answered. He conferred with three of his fellows over a jug.

The four of them spread out in a loose formation. One of them—not the fullback—called signals. "Thirty-seven, fourteen, sixty-two, twenty, hipe!" The jug flew between his legs. The fullback caught it, rolled over on his back and began gulping, gurgling and guffawing all at the same time. The other three, echoing her rebel yell, made an onside rush for the blonde.

"Touchdown!" she squealed when they reached her, stretching her legs wide and pointing the toes toward the sky. "Here's that good ol' field goal kicker. And now for the point," she added, eyeing the stiffest of the three unsheathed peckers.

The kicker placed it right between the goal posts. The blonde grabbed the other two stiffs, one in each hand, and hung onto them as she wrapped her long, golden legs around the kicker's hips and started to bounce on that glorious bottom of hers. "Whoo-ee!" she exulted. "Ain't nothin' like the playin' of the game if'n it's done right!"

"Ain't no way I can do it wrong!" the kicker panted. To prove it, he got his hands under her vibrating bottom and stood up, lifting her with him. Supporting her, he marched her around the goal posts, his large, brutal-looking, uncircumcised prick pumping in and out of her foaming quim all the while. Squealing, matching his rhythm, slapping wetly against his pelvic bone, the long, luscious blonde somehow managed to maintain her tight grip on the pricks of the two other jocks while all this was going on. Indeed, she did more than hold them. She actually frigged them in cadence with the balling of the kicker.

The kicker laid her back down on the ground. He bent her legs double and bent himself over her flushed, quivering ass and buried his cock to the hilt in her clutching pussy. Now he was fucking her in earnest. And now she was jerking off the other two guys with a vengeance.

Their balls swelled up. Their eyes glazed over. It was easy to see that they were on the verge of coming.

I could empathize. I wasn't even in the scene, and it had me horny as a stallion when the mares are in season. My cock had lost its cool and kept trying to poke holes in my underwear as I watched.

"Harder, kicker!" the blonde gasped. "An' y'all put more spin on it, hear now?"

"How's this?" His massive, hairy ass moved as if an earthquake had struck as his cock made some corkscrew motion deep inside her.

"Y'all do that again! I do believe my clitty's 'bout to bust!" She wrapped her legs around his neck. Her bountiful bottom bounced off the turf and rose high with deep, thrusting movements to match his. "Gettin' there! Gettin' there!" Her blonde head swiveled from right to left and back again. "How you boys doin'?"

"Cain't hardly wait!"

"My balls is 'bout to bust!"

"Kicker? Thank y'all can put it to me now?"

"Yep! Here she goes!"

The kicker's cock slammed down. The blonde's cunt shot up. They met and hung in midair, vibrating and humming as he shot his load of cream high up inside her and she rode the crest of her responding orgasm. At the same moment, she did something with her hands so that both the guys she'd been frigging began coming at the same time. Laughing excitedly, still coming, the blonde aimed their spouting peckers so that their jizzum squirted all over the kicker's ears from both sides.

"Hot damn!" Their spurtings waning to two dribbles, the pair of friggees fell on the grass roaring with laughter.

Still holding on to the comet-tail of her orgasm, the blonde echoed their guffaws with a trilling giggle of her own.

The kicker flopped out of her and sat down hard on his haunches. "Shee-it!" His hands went to his ears and came away sticky. "What for'd you go an' do that? Y'all know I've got 'nuf trouble with my ears as it is. Shee-it! Now I'll never hear them goddam signals!"

"But wasn't it worth it, Leroy? Truth, now!" The blonde wiggled her pussy at him.

"Shee-it! Y'all ask me the nex' time I boot for forty or more! Right now, I earned me a drank. An' I need a towel." He started back towards where the other jocks were sitting on the sidelines boozing and smoking pot. The other two followed him.

"Hey," the blonde called. "Send one of them

38

fellers back with a towel for me. I ain't none too neat 'n' shiny here myself."

A moment later the fullback was walking towards her with a towel in one hand and a new jug in the other. His hard-on preceded him like a flagpole sticking out of a window and waiting for a parade. The towel was white, his straining pecker was red, and his balls were more than a little blue from watching and waiting. Red, white and blue. Very patriotic. "I am rightly primed to fuck for Old Glory!" he told his teammates over his shoulder.

"Now, Jeeter, I rightly have to give it a rest first," the blonde cautioned as he reached her. "That Leroy, he left it a mite sore."

"Sure 'nuf, honey. Y'all know I'm the soul of consideration." He knelt between her legs and began to gently dab at her pussy with the towel.

"With a hard-on like one o' them Greek satyrs!" She took the towel from his hands, spread the lips of her quim wide and wiped briskly.

"I do rightly seem to have a problem here." The fullback bent his head and licked one of her red berry nipples with a long, wickedly thick tongue.

"Jeeter! You know my titties is my most generous zone! Oh, my Lord! I can feel that right down to my curly toes!"

Encouraged, Jeeter took a healthy amount of her breast into his mouth and sucked on it. The blonde's hands closed over the back of his neck and she began rocking back and forth on her haunches. "Land's sake!" she gasped. "Land's sake! How can a body ache so from havin' her pussy reamed out by a big cock an' at the same time want to get it on again! Land's sake!"

"Knowed you'd feel that way!" Jeeter pushed her over on her back and tried to mount her. Now his hairy balls looked the color of a cloudless sky at midday.

"No! Y'all wait!" The blonde pushed him off her. "You do me now, I'll just 'bout die!"

"Then what—?!"

"Don't y'all worry none now. I ain't gonna leave you in this disgraceful condition. Jeeter, you just lean against them goal posts an' stick your pecker out now." When he complied, she got on her hands and knees in front of him.

Her tongue snaked out and laved one of his swollen, hairy balls. Jeeter groaned and closed his eyes. The blonde kissed his other ball and then sucked it into her mouth between pursed lips. Her teeth snarled some of the thick, tangled black hair covering the ball and Jeeter groaned louder. The blonde crouched down lower and fondled one of her full, swaying breasts with her hand as she pushed Jeeter's balls aside with her nose and contrived to kiss the ridge of flesh behind them and between his legs.

"Kiss my ol' cock!" Jeeter begged. "Lick it! Suck it!"

The blonde laughed a low, knowing, throaty laugh. Her berry-nipple was red-hot and quivering in her hand. She ran the tip of her tongue along the length of Jeeter's aroused prick. She repeated the movement on both sides, then top and bottom. Then she took the swollen, wedge-shaped tip of his thick cock between her pouting lips. As she tasted it, her proud, pert ass, jutting and widespread, described small, hungry circles in the mote-swirling beam of the spotlight.

Her hand fluttered from her panting, perspiring breast to the bottom of the blonde mound between her legs. She touched herself there very tentatively. She winced. Nevertheless her trembling hand remained lightly pressed there as she opened her mouth wider and sucked Jeeter's cock more deeply inside it.

With half the shaft buried in her craw now, the blonde began making swallowing movements deep in her throat. At the same time her tongue was making eager, earthy slurping noises, and her lips were smacking rhythmically, and her head was moving back and forth with the sucking of Jeeter's cock. Her gleaming butt was stabbing the air with short, hard, jerky movements.

One of the onlookers detached himself from the group and approached Jeeter and the blonde. He looked smaller and lighter than the others—about five-foot-nine, maybe one hundred sixty-five pounds. He moved quickly and smoothly, like a split end, his hands automatically getting ready to receive and hold onto a pass. His naked cock was thin and not too long—kind of puny-looking compared to the bludgeons of the others.

When he reached the couple at the goal posts, he cupped the blonde's wild and wobbly ass between his deft, pass receiver paws. Alarmed, she spit out Jeeter's cock and craned to look over her shoulder. When she saw who it was, an expression of relief spread over her face.

"Y'all can put it where the sun never shines, Little John. That should feel right nice whilst I'm doin' Jeeter here."

"Why cain't I screw like Leroy done?"

"Now Little John, I have paid you a compliment! Ain't hardly anybody I let do me in my bottom. An' you bein' a mite undersized, an' me bein' so very, very tight there, why, it'll work out just right for both of us. Now you do what I say, Little John. Jeeter here's gettin' impatient, an he's full of shine. He loses that temper of his, they gonna be pitchin' your passes into a pine box."

Little John separated the two halves of the shimmering flesh-globe in his hands and inserted his thin, hard prick there. The blonde took Jeeter's glistening cock back in her mouth. Jeeter's fingers tangled in her hair and he shoved it so far down her throat that his puffed up hairy balls were bouncing against her hard-sucking lips.

The blonde breathed heavily through her nose as she sucked. The hand between her legs tickled her clitty lightly and played with Little John's immie-sized balls at the same time. Little John was holding onto her bucking hips and riding up and down on her thrashing ass like a bronco-busting cowboy.

I heard myself groan. I wished one of those moonshine jugs had come my way. I needed a drink. Or Stephanie. Or both!

"Whoo-ee!" Jeeter grabbed the blonde by the ears and slammed into her mouth. Her lips opened and his balls momentarily disappeared. "WHOO-EE!"

"WHOO-EE!" Little John echoed. His feet left the ground and he balanced his weight on the stiff, thin pecker buried in the blonde's bunghole.

"WHOO-EE!" The blonde's cry was silent, but somehow I knew it was the loudest of all.

She had to swallow quickly as Jeeter's lotion gushed down her throat. Also she had to keep the cheeks of her ass clenched tightly together to suck in all of Little John's lotion because he was thrashing so wildly on top of her as he came. She couldn't bring herself off with them when they came, however. I suppose it was because her pussy still hurt too much. Nevertheless, she was still trying, still tickling her clitty, when Jeeter and Little John both fell away from her exhausted.

"Y'all leave the jug," she instructed Jeeter when they dragged back to the sidelines.

He left it. She took a deep drag from it and swished it around inside her mouth. She was rinsing her mouth out after Jeeter, but at the last minute she thought better of it and swallowed the combination of moonshine and man-cream. Why not? She'd already swallowed everything else he'd had to offer. Resting, she drank from the jug until it was empty. Then she sat up and surveyed the sidelines. "I reckon I can handle three more of you degenerates 'fore we call it a night," she challenged.

"Thought your pussy was too sore." The answer came floating back.

"I'm just plain too horny to fret 'bout that. Y'all come on over here an' I'll show you."

The first one to take her up on her offer was a linebacker with a slow, slouching technique of a

43

determined gorilla. He set the blonde on her stomach and did her doggie-style from behind. He was casually brutal, but she didn't seem to mind. She came right along with him, squealing like a stuck pig while he emitted his great, wheezing gorilla roars.

A gentler giant followed him. He sat on the grass with his stilt-like legs outstretched and positioned the blonde on his lap. The thigh-muscles he usually used to outrun pass receivers bounded against her springy bottom while he squeezed her breasts with hamlike hands usually used to bat balls from the clutch of the opposition and fucked her with an eager cock more used to curling up inside jock straps. Primed now, made more excited with each succeeding lay, the blonde spread her pussy over his lap like a lady pirate tumbling jewels from a booty-chest. Later she slapped her gushing quim down hard on his sinew-jumping thighs and came just before he filled her with his pot-prolonged discharge.

"Phew!" She lay on her back panting, but not dissuaded. "Next!" she called. "Y'all hear me? Next!"

A short, powerfully built man with wide shoulders and narrow hips and a cock like a donkey's swaggered over to her. He pushed her over on her back, sprawled over her and shoved his large, rigid dong up her cunt. He had a behind that looked like a craggy anvil, but it pounded up and down over her more like a determined hammer.

As I stood watching them going at it, his predecessor, the guy with the lope-legs and the

44

pass-spoiling hands, spied me and came over. "Now y'all ain't with our team." Despite the words, his tone wasn't unfriendly.

"No, I'm not."

"But y'all are enjoyin' the show." He grinned.

"Yes, I am."

"Hell, long as you're here, even if you ain't with the team, it don't hurt to be hospitable. Y'all want a piece of the action?"

I thought about it. "I'd like to," I said honestly. "But the fact is I'm here to see somebody and it's kind of important."

"That a fact? Who you lookin' for?"

"A quarterback named Terry Niemath. You know where I might find him?"

"Terry Niemath?" A big grin broke over his face. "Shoot! Ain't nothin' easier. Right there." He pointed.

He was pointing at the couple wrapped around each other and straining under the goal posts. I looked at the grinding anvil ass and remembered the short, powerful build and wide shoulders. Yeah! There was even a passing resemblance to Joe Namath. The guy sure looked like he might be the kind of quarterback Rhino Dubrowski said he was. "Thanks," I told my grinning informant.

I watched as he banged his way to a climax. Yeah. Great concentration. Really good moves. He grabbed the blonde's breasts and twisted them cruelly. He had aggressive hostility too. No doubt about it, I thought, as they came together writhing and snarling. If he could only pass and run, he had all the makings of a star quarterback.

Giving him a minute to recover from his exertions, I thought about the problem which seemed to be weighing so heavily on Rhino's mind as to drive him to drink. I'd been right. Rhino was exaggerating the difficulty. Terry Niemath might be gay, but he was also obviously bi. Hell, if he didn't dig women, he could never have balled the blonde so enthusiastically. All we had to do was throw more blondes at him and make sure he stayed in line in the locker room. Hell, I'd have a talk with him. When he realized what was at stake, how he was going to play for a pro team, he'd surely straighten out. Yeah. The right kind of talk should do it. Problem solved!

I walked over to where the couple was sitting side by side on the grass. They'd gotten their breath back and were sharing a beer and a cigarette. I dropped down beside them with a smile. "Terry Niemath," I said, "I want to have a talk with you."

"Well, now, I do declare!" the short-haired blonde with the big boobs with the berry nipples replied. "Y'all are the first man all night who wanted to *talk* with me!"

Anvil-ass snorted through his beer.

I looked from one to the other of them and back again. "You're Terry Niemath?" I said to the blonde, my stomach dropping like iceberg time for the *Titanic*.

"Sure 'nuf, honeychile. Now just what is your problem?"

"My problem . . ." My problem was *not* solved. My problem was just beginning!

CHAPTER THREE

We changed at Atlanta for the non-stop jet to San Francisco. Terry Niemath scrambled into the window seat. I sat in the middle, Rhino on the aisle. We hadn't been able to get seats together on the plane out of Little Rock, and making connections had been a mad scramble at the world's largest and most screwed up airport, so this was really my first opportunity to discuss the situation with Rhino.

"When you told them in San Francisco that there was a sex problem, you really did mean a *sex problem!*" I had turned away from Terry and spoke in a low voice so she couldn't hear.

"It sure as excreta ain't just gender," Rhino replied glumly.

"Whoo-ee! I surely do love jets!" The blonde quarterback made a bid for our attention. "They're so big! An' they make me feel so horny!"

"Everything makes her feel that way," Rhino

47

sighed. "It's not just that she's female. It's also that when it comes to coitus she ain't got no quitting sense."

"Is today the first time you've ever flown?" I turned back to Terry, trying to be polite.

"First time in a jet. I hopped 'round Arkansas an' Tennessee in them little planes, but comin' from Little Rock this mornin', that was my first time in one of these here big, sexy mothers."

"Good afternoon, ladies and gentlemen," the intercom crackled. "This is Captain Corcoran, your pilot on the flight from Atlanta to San Francisco this afternoon."

"He surely does have a ee-rotic voice," Terry sighed.

What I heard in the voice was clear blue eyes, a square jaw, and a touch of grey at the temples—all those intrepid hallmarks an insecure passenger looks for in the pilot of an airliner since Duke Wayne died—but, then, maybe that was the same thing Terry was talking about.

"That's exactly the fecal attitude I mean!" Rhino told me.

"We've completed taxiing up the runway and we'll be taking off in just a minute," Captain Corcoran announced. "Our stewards and stewardesses will now check to make sure that all seat belts are securely fastened."

Terry had her pea coat spread over her lap so our steward had to lean across me and reach under it to check on her seat belt. A look like that of a cat who has just discovered leftover tuna fish in the garbage pail spread over her face. She smiled meltingly at

48

the steward and pinned his hand between her legs under the pea coat. His face was brick red by the time he managed to extricate himself.

"I just go absolutely ape over dudes in uniforms," Terry announced to the cabin at large.

"Our cohabitating luck! We couldn't get a stewardess!"

The plane took off. Terry stared out the window at the discharging jets and moaned low in her throat. The sight obviously jazzed up her libido.

"Aside from her promiscuity," I said in a low voice to Rhino, "how did you ever figure on getting around the fact that this great quarterback discovery of yours is female?"

"I thought I might try passing her off as a guy," Rhino mumbled.

"Really?" I glanced at Terry. Her breasts were large, delectable fleshy mounds spilling out of the carelessly buttoned work shirt she was wearing. "No way!" I told Rhino flatly.

"It was worth a shot," he insisted stubbornly. "I didn't say I was sure it would work. That's why I pressured them to send you down to Little Rock, Steve. I wanted to test it out on someone I could trust not to blow the whistle on me if it fizzled. I was going to let you see Terry play and if you couldn't tell it was a girl, why, then you'd be sold. You'd help me pull it off in California. But then," he sighed, "you went to the stadium and caught her balling and that was the end of that."

"Football is a contact sport," I reminded him. I took another quick look at Terry's boobs out of the corner of my eyes. "It's played at close quarters."

"With a chest protector and a loose jersey, she's all flattened out. Nobody could feel anything. With that short blonde hair, Terry could be a home-grown Viking from Minnesota."

"Not with a luscious butt like hers, she couldn't!"

"I worked out a way to change the shape of that with an ace bandage and tape."

"Bourbon's turning your brain to mush, Rhino," I told him. "You wouldn't have fooled me or anyone else past the first play."

"Then you don't think we could maybe pass Terry off as a guy in California," he wheedled.

"Not even in California," I assured him. "Not even in Southern California. Not even in Beverly Hills."

"Defecation! What am I gonna tell the Stonewall management?"

Before I could field that one, I was distracted by the very warm long fingers of a female hand on my thigh. "I'm gettin' bored," Terry Niemath complained. "Why don't y'all pay some attention to me, Mr. Victor, steada just to Mr. Dubrowski?"

"Call me Steve." I automatically reject formality.

It was a big mistake with Terry. She took it as an invitation to familiarity. "All right, Steve." Her long quarterback fingers dipped between my legs and stroked the sensitive inner surface of my thigh through my pants.

"How'd you get into football in the first place, Terry?" I removed her hand from between my legs,

50

patted it, and replaced it in her lap.

"I was standin' on a street corner crotch-watchin' with a girl friend one day. Along comes these two jocks wearin' jerseys with numbers an' tossin' a football back an' forth. One of 'em, he was what you'd call a real ten. Say bulge! Mmm-mmm! So I said somethin' I guess I hadn't oughta, an' this dude, he got all frazzled. That made me laugh, which I guess I also hadn't oughta, an' he got so mad that he bounced the football right off my poor head. Hard! I seen every star they is an' a few of them comets to boot. Well, that surely made me mad, too—madder 'n a wet hen too long 'thout a rooster! So what I done, I took that ol' football an' I just throwed it as far as I could, which is a whole lot further than anybody else in Little Rock could throw a football. An' that there's how a football star done got herself born." Terry put her hand back in my lap and squeezed my groin.

I caught her hand and pinned it between both of mine for safe keeping. "But how did you actually start playing?" I asked her.

"Them two boys, they invited me down to where they was scrimmagin' come the followin' Sunday. A pickup game, you know? Whoever shows pretty much gets a chance to play. Well, they covered my melons an' put me in at quarterback as a joke, I guess. Only it turned out I was so good it wasn't funny. Next thing you know, I was playing regular on Sundays all over Arkansas and Tennessee."

"But didn't the guys you played against realize that you were a female?"

"Didn't seem to bother them none." Terry's

wink was worthy of a bought-and-paid-for Senator interrogating an organized crime biggie.

"Still, what about the rules?"

"Now, just what rules is that, Steve honey?"

"The rule ain't been written could stop Terry here from coitus-ing her fundament off given the chance," Rhino interjected.

Terry wriggled agreement. One of her lovely bright red berry nipples waved at me from inside the work shirt. I gave my eyes permission to roam over her voluptuous body.

"She doesn't look like she weighs one-thirty-nine," I observed to Rhino. She was tall like Stephanie, and about her build too. Stephanie weighed about one-twenty-eight and was always trying to diet off five pounds of absolutely superb pulchritude.

"This chick's in great physical shape, really solid. There's muscles you'd never dream about under that gorgeous flesh. Not an excess pound! Still, one-three-nine is right. You could weigh her yourself."

"Please do, Steve." Terry purred. "Please do weigh me."

"I'll take Rhino's word for it." I ignored the innuendo. "You just don't look like you're carrying that many pounds."

"I'm big-boned." She licked her lips. "Are you big-boned, sugah?"

"We have leveled off at thirty-five thousand feet." Captain Corcoran's announcement over the PA saved me from having to respond. "Passengers

52

may remove their seat belts. Stewards and stewardesses will commence serving lunch."

"Excuse me, Ma'am, would you like some lunch?" the steward was back, distracting Terry's attention from me.

"Why, you darlin' man, I most surely would." The eye-batting she laid on him was right out of *Gone With The Wind*.

"Let me put your tray table down for you, Ma'am."

"You do that, sugah."

As he unfastened the tray table and lowered it over her lap, Terry contrived to capture his hand again. His face was only inches from mine and I could see the wild, helpless look of a trapped stag in his darting eyes. I could only imagine what Terry must be doing with his hidden hand. "I have to serve lunch," he pleaded.

"Y'all put lunch on hold, angel." She writhed in her seat and the color rising from the steward's neck to his forehead went from red to purple.

"I don't have time!" he wailed.

"Why, you surely do, darlin'." Terry closed her eyes. Time ticked by with the steward frozen into position. At last a long, contented moan escaped Terry's moist lips. "See, sugah, I knew you had time."

The steward fled. There was a clatter of out-of-control dishes from the galley. Later, when lunch was served, he was nowhere to be seen. A stewardess brought our rubberized club steaks and confetti salads.

"Now whatever do you suppose happened to that

nice boy?" Terry wondered.

"Internal combustion," I guessed. "He self-destructed."

"Why, Stephen, you silver-tongued flatterer, you!" She knocked the mucilaginous cheesecake into my lap, groping me. "How did y'all know I'm just a willin' fool for compliments?"

I evaded her by turning my body on one hip and facing Rhino. "I'm going to take a nap," I decided.

"You do that, honey." She patted my butt and left her hand there. The hand moved intimately a few times, but when I didn't respond, she became bored. "I have to go to the necessary," she announced.

Rhino and I got out of our seats to let her pass. She groped both of us successfully, and then she was gone. I stretched out on my seat again, meditating to relieve the tumescence of the organ strangling in my jockey shorts.

With flaccidity, after a bit, came sleep. Not for long, though. My stomach woke me serving notice that the plane was suddenly plunging earthward. As I shot up in my seat, my fellow passengers were already reacting.

"Oh, my God!"

"We're going to crash!"

"I knew I should have flown Braniff!"

"We're all going to die!"

"So flight insurance is for suckers, huh, Joe?"

"We are! We are going to crash!"

"Didn't Momma tell you to go before, Herbie? Now look!"

"Holy shit!"

"Repent! Repent, and ye shall be saved!"

"Holy excreta!"

The last to speak, just before the plane pulled out of the dive and righted itself, was Rhino Dubrowski. A moment later, when our original steward reappeared jogging down the aisle, Rhino grabbed him. "What's going on?" he demanded.

"Nothing to worry about, sir." As he spoke, the aircraft pointed its right wing towards the ground and side-slipped vertically for another thousand feet.

The movement caught the steward by surprise. Clutching for support, he ended up sprawled across Rhino's lap. "Nothing to worry about?" Rhino clung to him, more terrified than he'd ever been in 'Nam. "What do you call that?"

"Mild turbulence, sir." The steward struggled to his feet. "Just a little mild turbulence." He continued down the aisle towards the control cabin. Before he reached it, the plane gave another sickening lurch and went into a spin.

From somewhere behind me a man called for help in a heartrending voice of pure terror. "Is there a priest on board?"

"I'm a priest, my son." The answer came calm as a June day in a Killarney meadow.

"I have a confession to make, Father."

"Yes, my son."

"I've never been unfaithful to my wife, Father, and now, dammit, it's too late!"

"Peace, my son. God will forgive you."

"Maybe, but I'll damn well never forgive myself!"

The dive leveled off. The cabin of the plane was horizontal again. Then it tilted backward as the plane started to climb to regain altitude.

Slowly, the panic in the cabin eased. The PA system made a sound like milk shpritzing breakfast cereal. This was followed by Captain Corcoran's voice—deep, experienced, mellow, confident.

"Ladies and gentlemen, it has been brought to my attention by one of our stewards that some of you are concerned by that little bit of bumpiness we've been experiencing. Now, I want to reassure you that there is absolutely nothing to be worried about. If anxiety is making any of you feel a wee bit sick, however, remember there are bags into which you may relieve your nausea inserted in the backs of the seats in front of you. But rest assured that there is nothing unusual in this turbulence. I personally have flown this route over one hundred and ten times, and I assure you that this flight is exactly like all the others."

Captain Corcoran's speech would have been most reassuring indeed had it not been immediately punctuated by his high-pitched, hysterical laugh. The next voice heard over the PA both explained the laugh and unhinged the jaws of Rhino and myself. "Now, lamb, that is such a crock! Y'all know you have never, ever had you a flight like this before!"

"Don't touch his—!" I recognized the scream of the steward.

"Look out for the—!" Another male voice which I assumed belonged to the co-pilot.

Once again the airliner started to plummet. The

56

voice which accompanied this latest maneuver belonged to Terry Niemath. "Oh, Corky, when I put your dingus to me, I just feel so weak and dizzy and my head—! Oh, my, how my head does spin!"

"Where did he say that throw-up bag was?" A plaintive woman's wail.

"The back of the seat in front of—!"

"I'm sorry!" Too late. "I'm so sorry!"

"Oh, shit! Why on me? Why me?"

"Why any of us?"

"Jehovah moves in mysterious ways his punishments to perform! Repent!"

"Oh, feces!"

It was like being on a roller-coaster. Just when you were sure it was all over, the ride leveled off. Only this time the plane was wobbling from side to side as it flew on its roughly horizontal path. This was not reassuring. Neither was the voice of Captain Corcoran when next we heard it over the PA.

"Steward! Steward! What the hell are you doing?"

"I'm taking command of this aircraft, sir."

"Lady, stop that for a minute. I've got to get this straightened out. Now, steward, what did you—? Ooh! God, lady, just wait one—! Ooh!"

"I am relieving you of command, sir, under Article Twenty-three, Section Sixteen-C of the Flight Attendants' Code. You're no longer fit to decide the course of this aircraft."

"Mutiny! Steward, this is mutiny! . . . Oh, God! Not *there!* I go all out of control when a woman touches me *there!* ... Mutiny, I—ooooh! That feels so *good!*"

"Not mutiny, sir. Article Twenty-three, Section Sixteen-C of the Flight Attendants' Code says that, if the pilot in charge of the aircraft shall lose control of his command faculties, or if he shall commit a breach of public morality which causes the passengers to lose faith in his father image, then that member of the crew in the control cabin who is next in the line of command shall relieve the pilot of his responsibilities and take over the aircraft."

"Steward, this is madness! ... Oh, Jesus! Not under my—! Yo-yo-yo! That feels *fantastic!* ... And it's not logical either, steward. How have I demonstrated loss of control of my command faculties for instance?"

"I'll tell you in a moment, sir. First, is this switch here the rudder stabilizer, sir?"

"Steward, are you checked out to fly this aircraft?"

"No sir. Now, to answer your other question about loss of control of command faculties, sir. With all due respect to your rank, sir, might I remind you of the incident earlier in the day concerning the mini-bottles of liquor. The johns were unavailable to passengers and crew for forty-five minutes while you personally conducted a search for the three missing bottles."

"Steward, the company holds me personally responsible in seeing that none of those mini-bottles of booze is filched. I was only doing my job."

"Perhaps, sir, but in the middle of a hurricane,

shouldn't you have been flying the aircraft instead of putting it on remote control and crawling around under the toilets?"

"Let me remind you, Mister, that you know nothing about the pressures of command!"

"Corky, y'all are spoilin' the rhythm. Pay attention! I keep gettin' my little ol' titty caught in this here instrument. What is this thang anyway?"

"It's an ashtray. . . . Steward, there has been no breach of the public morality. Now get out of my control cabin!"

"Could y'all pull out your pecker an' then stick it back in my pussy, sugah, so I can scrunch down an' give better head to this here co-pilot?"

"I do believe that substantiates my case, sir."

"Nonsense! *Public* morality! And it has to cause the passengers to lose faith in my father image! . . . Oh, God! Will you look at that ass move! Is that a thing of beauty? Twirl it, lady! Go-go-go! . . . Nothing public about the privacy of the control cabin, so how could the passengers lose faith?"

"I anticipated that objection, sir. That's why I turned on the PA system. I wanted to be sure there would be witnesses for the Board of Inquiry."

"You turned on the—! Ah-ah-ah! Stop-stop-stop!"

"Yes, sir."

"Now, you listen to me, steward. Even if there were any excuse other than mutiny for this action, you would not be the one to undertake it. The co-pilot is next in the line of command after me. The only one in this cabin authorized to relieve me, therefore, is the co-pilot."

"Ordinarily that would be true, sir. But not in this case."

"Why not?"

"Because the co-pilot is incapacitated, sir."

"What's the matter with him?"

"He passed out soon as my lips touched it," Terry piped up. "I declare, it was too much for the poor boy."

"Don't you think you should stop doing it then?" the pilot suggested.

"Ain't hurtin' him none." Terry disagreed, giggling. "An' I surely do enjoy it."

"Steward!" Captain Corcoran proclaimed. "I'm taking those controls back!"

"No sir! I'm flying this plane!"

"Don't do that!" Captain Corcoran shouted. "Don't! It's dangerous!" His mounting concern was obvious over the PA. "We'll lose control! We'll go into another spin! We'll cra—!"

This time, most of us were braced. Most, but not all. One very young and attractive stewardess was flung sprawling into the aisle, her uniform skirt well up over her hips.

"Dear Lord! That poor girl isn't wearing any panties!"

"Please, sir! Keep your hands to yourself!"

"Yeah! Get your paws off her! I saw her first, Father!"

"You have your wife, my son."

"I should live so long."

"So should we all!"

"What would the Pope say?" the stewardess wailed.

60

"I'm sure I don't know. I don't speak Polish."

The stewardess fought her way to one of the johns and locked herself in as the plane once again righted itself.

"Pilot to control tower. Pilot to control tower." It was the steward's voice. "Request landing instructions."

"Just follow the radar beam in, Captain Corcoran," the control tower replied.

"Negative, control tower. This is not Captain Corcoran. This is an inexperienced pilot at the controls. I don't know how to follow a radar beam. Request manual landing instructions. Repeat, request manual landing instructions."

"Where is Captain Corcoran?" the control tower wanted to know.

"I have relieved him of command because of erotic instability. He is tied to the bulkhead. He is also gagged."

"Don't y'all just adore bein' trussed up an' all? I mean, bondage is such fun."

"Who was that?" the control tower wanted to know.

"A passenger. She's seeing to it that Captain Corcoran remains calm."

"Oh. Well, where is the co-pilot?"

"He's unconscious."

"What caused him to lose consciousness?"

"An attack of fellatio."

"What?!"

"Look, there really isn't time to explain it now. I have to land this aircraft. Will you please give me

61

landing instructions?"

"Roger. Turn thirty degrees and start your approach. . . . That's it . . . Very good! . . . Now bank . . . gently . . . gently . . . Let down your flaps . . . That's it . . . You're doing fine. Now your landing gear . . . good, good . . . Now, turn ninety degrees . . . turn ninety degrees! . . . TURN NINETY DEGREES, DAMMIT! . . . NEVER MIND! PULL UP! PULL UP! PULL UP ON THE STICK! . . . Jesus! What happened?"

"I don't know." The steward sounded like a balloon with the air let out. "I just froze. I froze at the controls."

"Well, get hold of yourself, man. Relax. We'll try it again."

"No!" The steward sounded panicky. "I can't relax! I'm afraid! I can't do it! I'll freeze again. I can't relax!"

"Jesus," the control tower realized, "you're too low for the passengers to bail out. You have to relax."

"I can't! I can't relax!"

"Wait a cotton-pickin' minute, fellas." It was Terry's voice, self-assured and sexy. "I can relax him. Y'all just leave it to me. Now, sugah, you just lean back an' close your eyes an' do how that there control tower says you should. All righty, control tower, I have found the zipper to his uniform trousers an' y'all can tell him what to do now."

"Start your approach again . . ."

"My! Such pretty skivvies! I never did see such pretty skivvies! Now where is that—? Ahh, here it is . . . Well, hello there, darlin'. You sure do stand up an' salute pretty now!"

"Bank slowly..."

"Mmmmm! Y'all do like to be kissed, don't you now?"

"Check your flaps..."

"An' I can surely tell you like to be kissed by the way y'all swell up."

"Check your landing gear..."

"Now, steward, honey, y'all let me suck this here wonderful pecker whilst you just relax an' enjoy it!"

"Now, turn ninety degrees..."

"Mmm! Mmm! I can tell you are *so-o-o* relaxed now! Mmmmm!"

"Now, a slow bank..."

"Ooh! You're so relaxed that y'all are goin' to come in my mouth right now. Wait! Let me get it all the way back in an' down my throat! Mmmmmm! Mmmmmm! MMMMMMMMMMMM-MMMMM!"

"Now just set her down easy..."

"HERE I COME!" the steward yelled.

It was a three-point landing.

CHAPTER FOUR

"The quarterback is a nymphomaniac!"

"I hate it when you talk that way." At the other end of the long distance line Stephanie Greenwillow's voice bristled with unsheathed feminist bayonets.

"But she is. She really is."

"Nonsense! There is no such thing as a nymphomaniac."

"Really? Well what do you call a girl who balls the whole football team in one night and then the very next day nearly cracks up an airliner because she has to have sex so much that she takes on the pilot, the co-pilot, and a steward?"

"In the first place, I don't call her a girl. I call her a woman. You got that, *boy?*"

"Oh, for Christ's sake, Stephanie—!"

"And in the second place, what do you call a man who has several women over the span of a day and a

64

half? I'll tell you what. A make-out artist! That's what you call him! A stud! You admire him. But when it's a woman, you call her a nymphomaniac! Really, Steve, I'd hoped you might have learned something from our relationship!"

"Oh, I did. I did. I learned how never to watch a Superbowl game."

"But you haven't." She ignored my interruption. "You're still a hopeless sexist!"

"That's right! Call me names! I call you up long distance from San Francisco to discuss my problems with you, because we do have this relationship, and you get on your women's lib high horse and call me names!"

"Did have!" Arctic fury. "Did have this relationship! Past tense! I am not going to fall into the trap of sacrificing my principles to keep from ruffling the feathers of some sexist male!"

"Okay, lady! If that's the way you want it!" I went on to tell her specifically where she could insert her principles. The instructions were to no avail. She hung up on me before I got to the really graphic and pithy part.

Steaming, I flung my clothes all over the fancy suite Charles Putnam had booked for me at the Mark Hopkins Hotel and dived into the shower. I stayed there a long time. Water therapy. Nothing like it for terminating relationships.

Later, not at all hungry and feeling more sorry than angry, I went up to the Top of the Mark for a drink. Sensitive to my mood, the headwaiter gave me one of the desirable window tables. From it I had a spectacular view, particularly of the bay when the revolving cocktail lounge brought it into sight. Drenched in romantic starlight, with a moon like an orange basketball hanging over it, the sparkling vista only added to my self-pity and feelings of loss. Stephanie had been special—infuriating, but special. I knew that there was no sense trying to call her back. Stephanie would have castrated her grandfather for *The Cause*. She'd never made any secret of just how expendable I was. So I sighed and stared out over the moonbeams at Fisherman's Wharf and assuaged my sorrow with a third scotch.

"Excuse me, sir." The headwaiter was at my elbow.

I looked up at him questioningly.

"We're filling up," he apologized. "I wondered if you would mind if this lady shared the table and view with you?"

It was on the tip of my tongue to say that I minded very much, that I treasured my solitude, on this evening particularly. Before I could speak, however, the young lady in question edged out from behind the headwaiter and smiled at me.

"Well, I do declare! If it isn't Mr. Steve Victor his very self. Hello, there," Terry Niemath greeted me.

"Ah, you know each other." The headwaiter was relieved. He held the chair out for her.

"Y'all don't mind, Steve, do you?"

"Of course not." I lied vehemently. "I'm glad of the company." I compounded the lie. Of all the female company I didn't feel like at this time, Terry Niemath's headed the list.

The waiter came and took her order for a boilermaker. He looked surprised. I could understand why. This was a different Terry from the other two occasions I'd seen her. On the first she'd been the very picture of a voluptuous libertine who wore her lust as unashamedly as if it were a Dior original covering her nudity. On the second she'd been a brazen hoyden in too-tight, faded jeans and bosom-flaunting work-shirt.

Now, by contrast, she was wearing a simple, inexpensive dress of the sort a Little Rock matron might wear to an evening meeting of the Garden Club. Her sleek, blonde hair was combed neatly back from her face and held in place by a barrette. The skirt of the dark print dress hung demurely to mid-calf, and the top was buttoned all the way up to a high V. Although it was obvious that she wasn't wearing a bra (I don't believe she owned one), her nipples were lost in the busy print and her large, high breasts neither panted nor swayed to draw attention to themselves. She looked attractive and young, but not particularly sensual or available.

"Y'all look like your pet spaniel just got run over," Terry observed.

Her perceptiveness surprised me. Before I knew it, I was telling her how I'd just split up with my woman friend. (I did not, however, tell her that the split-up had been precipitated by my labeling her, Terry, a nymphomaniac.) She listened sympathetically, asked questions about Stephanie, the length of the relationship, and the qualities that attracted us to each other.

"Sex surely is important," she observed in

response to my listing that as primary. "Y'all may not believe this, Steve, but I used to be real attracted to you that way."

Used to be? I'd barely known her two days. "You mean you're not attracted to me any more, Terry?"

"Nope. Oh, I like you as a person well 'nuf. But you don't make me lust like at first. You see, Steve, it's the way I am. If'n I know another woman rejected a fella, why, then he just loses all appeal for me."

"You mean I don't appeal to you any more?"

" 'Fraid not."

A surge of desire started down around my toenails and bubbled up to my sinuses. Yesterday Terry had wanted me and I hadn't been terribly interested. Now she didn't want me any more. Immediately, I knew that I had to have her!

I burned for her! Under the low table my instant erection was threatening to become a tilting embarrassment. My eyes devoured the sweep of her breasts. My brain reeled with the memory of her long arching legs, her hips in action, her pneumatic *derriere*—and with the effects of my fifth scotch.

"But we can still be friends," I said carefully, cunningly, my mind already beginning to seethe with diabolically contrived plans to get her into bed. Rejection was not something that I, Steve Victor, the man from O.R.G.Y., could willingly accept from a (Up yours, Stephanie!) nymphomaniac.

"Of course, darlin'."

"Then why don't we go down to my room and have a friendly nightcap," I suggested brightly.

"I do believe we have both had more than

enough to drink," Terry parried smoothly.

"Etchings?"

"My great-granddaddy warned me all 'bout that."

"Then how about just plain, friendly sex?"

"Now, Steve, I already 'splained how I feel 'bout you in that department."

"But you said we were friends."

"We are."

"Well, what are friends for?"

"To provide y'all with a shoulder to cry on when your lady friend gives you the gate."

Some nymphomaniac!

"How about taking a drive," I suggested desperately. Charles Putnam had arranged for a Mercedes 480 SL rental car to be waiting for me at the airport when we arrived. Now it was stashed in the garage under the hotel.

"Why, that'd be real nice. I'd love to see San Francisco by night."

My contriving to get Terry Niemath into a car was really a form of sexual regression. Five scotches had reduced me to the basic stratagems of the years of my puberty. Hell, the old 'Let's go-for-a-ride' ploy had worked on Euphremia Hossenpfeffer when I was sixteen years old, so why not on Terry now?

Like Terry, Euphremia had had what in those days we called "a reputation". (Fie, Stephanie Greenwillow! Fie, and *plotz!*) Of course, back then, I had been a virgin, and now I was the Man from O.R.G.Y., but the urge was just as strong. (Rejection makes me horny; I can't help it.) Terry, like

Euphremia, was being what I chose to regard as 'coy', but a quick spin in the moonlight climaxed by a parking interlude at a carefully chosen D.E.S. should take care of that.

I followed a zigzag, semi-scenic route from Nob Hill to Russian Hill to the Golden Gate Bridge. It didn't provide the greatest views of San Francisco but, at that time of night, it drew less traffic than Chinatown, Fisherman's Wharf, and Telegraph Hill in the other direction. Besides, I wanted to get across the bridge to Sausalito, where I figured I might find a suitable parking spot somewhere in the hills overlooking the waterfront. If you can't pull off a seduction in the hills of Sausalito, you might as well give up on the West Coast altogether.

"Lordy! Isn't that the most beautiful sight y'all ever did see!" Each step of the way—Russian Hill, the Golden Gate Bridge, the Sausalito waterfront itself—Terry had been making comments like that. This one, however, was certainly justified. I had taken the high ground and found us a deserted scenic overlook on top of a bay-side cliff that provided a truly spectacular view of lit-up San Francisco across the water.

"Romantic, too." Hell, how subtle do you have to be at my age with five scotches inside you?

"Yes," she sighed. "It surely is."

Some such dialogue had once been my cue to kiss Euphremia Hossenpfeffer, she of the pudgy thighs and questionable "reputation". Such signals aren't subject to change, are they? I put my arms around Terry Niemath and pressed my lips to hers.

Deja vu!

"I don't want you to get the wrong idea about me," Euphremia Hossenpfeffer had told me on that long-ago night when I had accompanied that first kiss with Seduction Step Number One (as outlined to me by my friend Murray Wiener, who was two years older than me, going to college, and who claimed to have been laid, thus already the man of the world I was panting to become), the forcing of the male tongue into the female mouth.

"Y'all don't get any wrong ideas now, hear?" Terry said as she released my tongue from between her lips.

"Of course not, just a friendly kiss between friends." I slid my hand down from her shoulder to the tilted missile-mounds of her breasts.

"I don't think I should let you touch me there, Stephen," Euphremia had protested. (But Murray had said she was 'hot to trot', and Murray had been a Man of the World.)

"I do thank y'all might be gettin' a wee bit too friendly." But the polyester of Terry's dress was thin and (unlike Euphremia) she wasn't wearing a bra, and the stiffness of her nipple belied her protest.

I kissed them again to still their objections.

"You surely do know how to kiss," Euphremia sighed. (How about *that*, Murray?)

"Y'all surely do know how to kiss real sweet an' friendly," Terry granted.

I played with their nipples through their clothing. (Seduction Step Number Two, courtesy of Murray Wiener.) Then I slipped my hand inside Euphremia's bra and Terry's dress and fondled their hot, bare nipples. (Step Three.) There wasn't much in the way of breast around Euphremia's, as I recall, but Terry's soft-but-firm mammaries more than made up for my earlier deprivation.

"Ohh!" Euphremia moaned. "I get so excited when a boy touches me naked there!" (Aha! She'd been touched there before! Her "reputation" was deserved! . . . See, Stephanie!)

"Playing with my naked nipples surely does make me squirm," Terry conceded. (A small, but significant sign of nymphomania reviving.)

I leaned over the stick-shift, bent my head and took their long, quivering nipples in my mouth. (Step Four.) My chin sank into the rhythmically rising and falling pillows of Terry's breasts and bumped against Euphremia's rib-cage. I used my lips and I used my tongue and I sucked. (Step Five a, b, and c.)

Euphremia gasped and dug her nails into the back of my neck. Terry gasped and dug her nails into the back of my neck. Euphremia began to pant noticeably. Terry began to pant noticeably. Euphremia squirmed and I could see the outline of her legs separating under her skirt. Terry, ditto.

I slipped my hand under the hems of their skirts. (Step Number Six. "Timing is crucial," Murray Wiener—the Alex Comfort of my heretofore sexually joyless teen years—had advised.) I kept sucking their nipples as I established beachheads just above the knees.

"I don't do anything below the waist!" (Aw, come on, Euphremia, what about your *"reputation"*?)

"Y'all are movin' into mighty dangerous territory for someone wants to just be my friend!"

("Step Six is usually where they try to stop you," Murray had warned. "The trick is not to let it throw you. They have to say it, but they don't really mean it. Just keep right on going and don't worry about it." I worried about it. "Suppose they yell 'Rape!' " When I worry, I worry good. "No sweat. You're underage." Wow! The things Murray had learned in college!)

I continued to suck nipples and grope thighs. Euphremia's pudgy ones and Terry's sleek, long, shapely ones were equally hot and trembly under my fingers. Each time I ran my tongue over their nipples, Euphremia's baby fat squeezed together and twin muscles jumped under Terry's flesh.

From under eyelids drooping with passion, both girls noticed the bulge distorting my pants and smiled that secret smile that women smile when acknowledging their power to narrow the male down to the demands of his erection. "It really isn't right for me to get you so aroused," Euphremia apologized. "A boy I know told me you can hurt yourself like that because I won't let you—you know." Terry was similarly sympathetic. "Y'all are goin' to have a terrible case of blue balls an' it'll be all my fault," she said sorrowfully.

I forgave both of them, kept right on licking, kissing and sucking nipples, and inched higher until I felt panty material—loose and surprisingly lacy in Euphremia's case, snug cotton bikini for Terry. My hard-on throbbed and jerked inside my pants. I had to restrain myself to keep from biting

73

down on the straining nipples in my mouth, I wa
so inflamed.

Euphremia's panties felt damp and slipper
Terry's panties were warm and wet and sucked i
tight against the swollen, open lips of her pussy.
pushed the tip of my middle finger against ther
rhythmically. (Step Seven.)

("Even through the panty material, you shoul
go for the clitty," Murray Wiener recommended.

"What's the clitty?" How are you going to lear
if you don't ask questions?

"You'll know it when you feel it.")

Murray had been wrong. I didn't know it when
felt it with Euphremia. As a matter of fact, to thi
day I've never actually been sure if I *did* feel it.
was a lot older and more experienced with Terry, o
course. Besides, her clitty was sticking right ou
there like a miniature hard-on. I rubbed it throug
her panties.

I pushed the panties aside. I dipped my middl
finger in the wells. I moved it in and out accordin
to the dictates of Step Eight.

"I shouldn't be letting you do this," Euphremi
panted.

"This here is a bad mistake!" Terry gasped.

My answer was the same to both of them. I too
their hand and wrapped it around the throbbing
cock tenting my pants. Both of them made a fis
and began moving it.

I pulled their panties down, dropped my head
between pudgy thighs and sleek thighs and kissed
their pussies. ("You won't be able to stop them
from fucking once you do that," Murray had

74

assured me . . . another of the astounding things learned in college!)

"Omigod! No boy ever did *that* to me before!" Euphremia's pussy squirmed under my tongue. (Her "reputation" had evidently not filled all the gaps in her experience.)

"Lick it, Steve! Kiss it! Suck it!" Terry was bouncing up and down on her beautiful ass, snapping at my tongue with the lips of her quim.

I undid my belt. I unzipped my fly. I pushed down my underwear and my pants. I wrapped their fists around my naked cock. And all the time I kept on eating their pussies, a maneuver which stilled my doubts they might have had about my unsheathing my outrageously elongated manhood.

The floor shift made matters a little tricky but, adolescent and man, I always was innovative. I slid to the floor on the passenger side of the gearbox and balanced on my hands. This way the top of my head was on the seat and my mouth was able to resume feasting on the quims. Also—and crucial at this point (although in truth Murray Wiener had never mentioned it)—my stiff cock stuck out exactly at lip level and probed demandingly.

"I never sucked a boy upside-down before!" That made two firsts for me with Euphremia.

"Mmm-mmm! There is nothin' as dee-licious as steamin' hard pecker!"

Euphremia's fleshy thighs had locked around my ears, shutting out all sound. I widened the entrance to her cunt with my tongue and kissed the sensitive pink flesh deep inside it. The inside of her pussy was tight and ridged and it moved up and down

75

grindingly as I frigged it with my tongue. Her own tongue was lapping at my balls, making hungry wet, smacking noises. Then her lips were around the head of my cock and her sandpaper tongue was licking up the early drops of jizzum leaking there. Finally she opened her adolescent mouth wide and sucked my thrashing cock deep down her throat. She sucked and swallowed greedily. We sucked in unison.

The muscles of Terry's inner thighs flexed and unflexed over my ears, creating an effect like holding a seashell near, then far away, and then near to one's ear. I was riding her clitty with my tongue now, and this so excited her that she had reached under her with one hand and had spread the cheeks of her beautifully molded bottom in order to play up her own anus. She had wonderful control of the muscles inside her cunt, and they rippled over my tongue, squeezing it as I licked her. She bent her head between my legs and licked the cleft of my behind and the underside of my balls. She sucked first one of the balls and then the other into her mouth and probed each with her tongue. Finally she licked the length of the shaft of my quivering pecker and kissed the tip, probing the hole there with her tongue-tip. She took the prick deep down her throat and squeezed it in unison with her pussy muscles squeezing my tongue.

Euphremia was sopping with honey in a way I hadn't known girls did. Terry was squeezing out her joy in thick, perfumed, oily little spurts. My balls were filling with jizzum. My mouth-immersed cock was straining and ready. It was tempting as hell to let go down those hungry throats, but neither then, nor now, was I about to let good old Murray Wiener down. Besides, the blood was rushing to my head. It was time for Step Nine.

I scrambled to an upright position. I pushed female thighs wide apart and raised female legs high for easier entry. I shoved my cock up the quims, one gloriously, adolescently tight, the other like a lemon squeezer equipped with wondrous womanly muscles. Flailing hands clawed at my buttocks. Frantic teeth sank into my shoulder. I slammed my prick in and out hard, my balls slapping against the hot, wet curve of writhing asses.

"Oof!" I exclaimed. "Oof! Oof! Oof!"

"You're hurting me!" Euphremia cried out.

"Lordy, Steve! This position is purely murder!"

Originally, it hadn't occurred to me that any other position was possible. Euphremia (she had a *'reputation'*, remember!) had introduced me to the more automotively sensible and comfortable seated-man-on-the-bottom position. I slid into it a lot more easily with Terry.

Spreading her pudgy thighs, Euphremia knelt between my legs on the seat and gently lowered herself onto my steel-hard, frothing cock. Terry, on the other hand, sat with her long legs stretched up my body with the angles waving over my ears. Terry definitely had the edge, if memory serves me right. Her position allowed for much deeper penetration.

"Touch me here!" Euphremia put my finger where I supposed her clitty was as she rode up and down my cock, her sparse bare breasts hanging out

77

from under the bra with the taut nipples beckoning the fingers of my free hand.

"Play with my no-no!" Terry guided my hand between the flushed and squirming cheeks of her behind as I sucked her stiff berry nipples and firm, large bullet breasts through the polyester of her dress.

(Hey, look, Murray. I'm fucking!)

"Does this feel good?" Euphremia licked my ear as she bounced up and down.

"Y'all like this, darlin'?" Terry twisted over my deeply imbedded prick in small, tight corkscrew circles.

"Yeah!" I told them. "Great! Keep fucking!"

I was straining so hard now that at no time did my bare bottom touch the car seat. My thighs were bathed with the lubrication of female passion. My balls were on fire and tingling with the mounting pressure for release. I opened my mouth wide and sucked in breasts—one entire, and one gloriously overflowing. I shoved my cock tonsilward with one last brutal, mighty thrust. I came! (Step Ten.)

"I came!" I announced to Terry, Euphremia and Murray Wiener. "Did you come?" I asked the first two, considerate from first to last.

"Yes. I did." Euphremia, at least, had the courtesy to lie. "The earth moved." She was, however, a little short on originality. "It was wonderful!" (Many years later I ran into Euphremia and we went to bed together for old time's sake. On that occasion she confessed to me that she had not had her first orgasm until one month after her twenty-sixth birthday, and then

78

only with a vibrator.)

"No, I surely did not!" Terry was annoyed. "Now don't y'all dare pull out now until I'm rightly through with you!" She twisted and squeezed and panted over my limpening dick until she finally let out a squeal, and—ball-wrenchingly—came.

When it was over, we shared a cigarette. "I guess you changed your mind, huh?" I couldn't resist needling Terry.

"Y'all thank so, huh?" She winked.

"What do you mean?"

But she only winked a second time. I had to be satisfied. It was all the explanation I was going to get.

We drove back to the Mark Hopkins. On the way, Terry asked me a question. "Who's Euphremia?"

"What?!" I was startled.

"Who's Euphremia?" she repeated. "When you came, you spit my breast out of your mouth, raised your head to the sky and brayed her name: Euphremia. Who is she?"

I winked at her. It was all the explanation she was going to get. Now we were even.

I pulled the car into the underground garage at the hotel. We took an inside elevator up to Terry's suite. I kissed her good night at the door and took another elevator up to my suite.

There was a note on my door to call the desk for a message. It was from Charles Putnam. He had left word for Rhino Dubrowski and me to be at Baroquian Orchard, a three-thousand-acre retreat for members of the Baroquian Club deep in the red-wood forests about eighty miles north of San Francisco, at noon the following day. We would meet there with Putnam and the other interested members of the group behind the Whittier Stonewalls. There were careful directions on how to drive there. There was an additional instruction to the effect that nobody was to come but the two of us. The meaning was obvious. They were planning to discuss Terry Niemath and they didn't want the quarterback to be present.

I stuck the instructions where I couldn't miss them when I dressed in the morning and went to bed. Five scotches and a good lay. I slept like a log.

The next morning, when I awoke, I had time to kill. I decided it would be a nice gesture to have breakfast with Terry before leaving her alone for the day. I took the staircase down to her room and knocked at the door.

My first knock went unnoticed, but my second one brought a muffled answer. "Y'all come on in."

I entered the sitting room. There was no one there. The door leading to the bedroom was closed. I walked over to it and knocked again.

"I said y'all could come right on in."

I entered. I looked. My jaw dropped.

"Steve, darlin'. Welcome to the party." Terry grinned up at me from her bed.

She was lying on top of the sheets. She was naked. There was a naked man on either side of her. One of them had his semi-erect penis resting between her voluptuous cheeks of her behind. The other was embedded in her pussy. Two bellhop caps perched side by side on the nightstand.

"Take off your clothes an' join us, darlin'."

80

"No, thanks." I backed out of the room.

Well, Stephanie? How about that? Is there still no such thing as a nymphomaniac?

CHAPTER FIVE

En route to the Baroquian Club's redwood retreat with Rhino Dubrowski, I was reminded of a time when I was a kid and my only erections came from inadvertent rubbing by a corduroy crotch and led nowhere. Back then, I was one of five founding members of an exclusive boys' club. We met in a cellar and debated the joys and consequences of masturbation and ejaculation (which none of us had experienced yet). Being an elite group, we had no one to question our expertise. Occasionally we measured our weenies against one another. We felt, as I recall, very manly.

This feeling was bolstered by barring from membership all boys who were too fat, were too puny, had pimples, wore glasses, always raised their hands with the answers in class, covered their heads when a ball was thrown at them, or lived outside the neighborhood. All girls, having no weenies, were blackballed by definition. Another reason for their exclusion was our need for masculine privacy to figure out just what we were going to do to them as soon as we got old enough to be able to do it. Sometimes, one of us would snitch his sister's bra and put it on and pretend to be a girl so we could act out these fantasies.

Our exclusivity was power. We were the 'ins'; they were the 'outs'; we were superior, and all the other poor *zhlubs* were inferior. I remember how delicious it was to intimidate and overawe the occasional guest a member was allowed to bring to meetings of our private club.

Now here I was on my way to being the guest of Charles Putnam at the ultra-exclusive Baroquian Club, where you not only had to be superior to be a member, you also had to be *grown up!* Wow! What an honor! I'd get to rub shoulders with really important guys who were 'in', who were expert in many grown-up fields, and who had lots and lots of power. They probably wouldn't measure their weenies against each other but, then, that's how it is when fellows grow up. They have to put childhood pleasures behind them. *Some* childhood pleasures, anyway. Others were still indulged at the Baroquian Club.

Like most people, I had first heard of the Baroquian Club when the California Fair Employment and Housing Department brought a suit charging them with sex discrimination. The legal action was taken because of the club's policy of not hiring anybody who lacked a penis. ("What have girls got there?" we used to wonder. "How can they stand it?")

The resulting publicity revealed that, in addition to discriminatory employment practices, the Baroquian Club, just like my boyhood club, barred all women from both membership and guest privileges. The Baroquians also excluded all blacks, Jews who were not either former Secretaries of State or former National Security Advisors, Italians who did not own casinos or run major automobile manufacturing corporations, and all other minority group members who were not board chairmen of one of the *Fortune Five Hundred*. The exceptions mentioned within these groups were, of course, not eligible for membership, but they were allowed guest privileges.

Unlike my club, the Baroquian Club did not discriminate against the obese, the spindly, the pimply, the near-sighted, the smart-asses, or the athletically uncoordinated. Indeed, most of the Baroquian Club membership seemed to fall into one or another of the categories my boyhood organization had blackballed. So it goes. One group's pariahs are another group's elite.

Their elite ranged in importance from former and present Vice Presidents and Presidents of the United States to oil company executives and bankers who regularly decided the Prime Rate. These select gentlemen awoke one morning to find that a Baroquian Club spokesman had revealed to the press the club tradition of holding frolics and staging shows in which the members dressed up as women. Such transvestite activity, he pointed out (not, however, in those words), required a suspen-

84

sion of inhibitions which would most certainly be hampered by the hiring of non-male menials. How, he asked the reporters man-to-man, could a fellow feel comfortable in pantyhose if he was to come under the eye of a gender trained from childhood to detect flaws in feminine dress? The Baroquian Club's male members, after all, were an executive group with tremendous responsibilities causing daily strain and pressure. Weren't they entitled to relax?

("There's nothing so relaxing," feminist Stephanie Greenwillow had remarked when she read this, "as slipping into a girdle and putting your feet up.")

It was shortly before noon when Rhino and I turned onto the access road leading to Baroquian Orchard. Driving between evenly-spaced rows of giant redwoods, we approached a high, chained iron gate. There was a guard booth outside. Two uniformed men holding shotguns brought us to a halt beside it.

"I'm Steve Victor, and this is Mr. Elmer Dubrowski," I told them. "We're guests of Mr. Charles Putnam. He's expecting us."

"One moment, sir." The first guard's politeness as he retreated to the booth and picked up a telephone for confirmation was cancelled out by the second guard's shotgun still held at the ready.

"Tight security," I remarked to Rhino.

"Tighter than a constipated Presbyterian center's anal cavity."

"You're expected, sir. Welcome to Baroquian

Orchard." The iron gates were opened, and we were waved on through.

As we followed the road winding beside the river up the mountainside, the redwoods gave way to gardens of sculpted flower beds and meadows being grazed by sheep and cattle. The last half-mile provided a view of rolling lawns, some with croquet setups; a beautiful, geriatrically banked golf course; tennis courts which, although carefully maintained, didn't look as though they got much use; and a selection of heated swimming pools, jacuzzis, and natural baths. Rising from these, on the tip of the mountain, overlooking the river on one side and the blue-green vista of the Pacific Ocean on the other, and framed by another careful planting of giant redwoods, stood the mansion-clubhouse of the Baroquians. Done in the baronial style of a Portuguese castle, its turrets and parapets were not so much reminiscent of San Simeon as an enlargement upon its vulgarity which nevertheless could not fail to impress a first-time viewer like Rhino Dubrowski.

"Holy fecal matter!" he exclaimed, massive jaw agape.

"Onward to the Crusades!" I responded.

"Huh?"

I didn't bother to explain. I pulled the rented Mercedes around the circular driveway to where a liveried footman waved me to a halt. When Rhino and I alit, he slid behind the steering wheel and, I presume, drove the car to where it was to be parked.

A second footman escorted us up the steps to the

huge, oaken castle door. Here he turned us over to an elderly gent who resembled a skinny penguin in his black and white formal butler's garb. "Mr. Putnam is waiting for you two gentlemen in the library," he informed us. "If you'll come with me, please."

We followed him on a safari through halls of Byzantine marble, trudging dutifully over polished redwood floors, eyeing Moorish tapestries and Dresden figurines and artifacts from looted Egyptian pyramids arranged on weavings from sacked Buddhist temples. All this was illuminated by the bright California sunlight streaming through the high, long castle windows. Here and there, an occasional original abstract print by Kandinsky provided a particularly jarring note. But the decor was such an incredible hodgepodge of all that money could buy that a critic would have been hard put to justify any criticism. Since the Medicis, artistic taste and moneyed indulgence have increasingly gone their separate ways.

"Hey, look!" A nudge from Rhino broke into my musings.

"Isn't that—?"

I looked. "Yeah," I agreed. "It is."

Walking towards us was a former President of the United States of America. As he came abreast of us, he craned his head to look at a display of prize-winning Ruth Orkin photographs taken from the window of her apartment on Central Park West. "Drop dead, New York!" he mumbled, stumbling as he popped his chewing gum. He shot us a sort of sheepish grin, ducked his head and continued on his way.

We rounded a corner and almost bumped into a world-famous evangelist coming down the hall. He was holding a Bible in front of him with both hands and paraphrasing it aloud. ". . . and Nelson begat Henry and Henry begat Zbigniew and Zbigniew begat Alexander and Alexander begat . . ." He passed out of our hearing.

"This way, gentlemen." Distracted, we had not been keeping up with our formally-garbed guide. Now, we performed a fast shuffle and fell into step with him. A few moments later, he stepped aside, so that we might pass through the doorway to the library.

It was a large room and, while there were murmurings from various groups which had arranged themselves around it, the atmosphere was, on the whole, quite hushed. Waiters in livery glided about on soundless ball bearings. Their trays held large snifters of brandy so rich in color as to create a positive aura of investment capital. The waiters themselves looked as if they had been selected by Central Casting to portray New England church elders in a period drama about Cotton Mather.

Across the room Charles Putnam rose to greet us—or, rather, rose and waited for us to cross the room and greet him. He was not much changed from the last time I had seen him. The grey flannel suit; the navy blue tie with the Old School design dotting it sparsely with grey; and the high, white, round-collared shirt all looked the same as always. Likewise the unflinching steel color of his hair and the noncommittal, blander greyness of his face. The years may have added a line or two to his frozen features, but they weren't pronounced enough to be read as evidence of any aging process. And his blue eyes were still as clear and sharp and friendly as diamond chips.

"Good to see you, Mr. Victor." His hand was an over-refrigerated flounder.

Rhino's presence rated only a brusque nod of acknowledgement. Putnam indicated that Rhino and I should be seated in deep, red plush arm-chairs. Three of them had been arranged about a small, round redwood table. Putnam sat in the third chair without disturbing the crease of his trousers and signaled a waiter. "Brandy, gentlemen," he suggested.

"I'd rather have scotch," I said, just to watch him grimace.

He took that in his stride but had trouble con-trolling the muscles dilating his nostrils when Rhino requested bourbon with a beer chaser.

"So how's the discrimination suit going?" I asked. There has always been something about Put-nam that pushes me into needling him when the op-portunity comes up.

"Could you lower your voice, Mr. Victor. I don't wish to distress our other members."

"The suit distresses them?"

"Of course. It threatens our traditions."

"Traditions..." I glanced around the mahogany-paneled room. Across from us, I spied the Secretary of Defense of the United States chat-ting over a plate of crackers and genuine Russian caviar with the president of a concern seeking a contract to manufacture atomic warheads for the

89

government. The chairman of the board of a major oil company being sued for an off-shore oil spill which had destroyed the recreation possibilities of two-thirds of a coastal state's beaches was lighting a genuine Havana cigar for the State Attorney General in charge of investigating the spill. A major national building contractor was sniffing rare Chinese brandy with the chairman of a Senate subcommittee considering his petition for a waiver of restrictions protecting the environment. "It's nice," I told Putnam, "that the club's traditions jibe so well with the members' self-interest."

"That is nonsense, Mr. Victor. Because we are a private organization and shun publicity, a myth has grown up that the Baroquian Club is a front for international power brokers, and that all sorts of high-level political and business deals are made here. Nothing could be further from the truth. In point of fact, it is a sanctuary from such concerns."

"I guess that explains why the membership includes at least one officer from forty of the fifty largest manufacturing concerns in the country, one director from twenty of the twenty-five largest banks, and one ranking executive from more than half of the nation's largest life insurance companies."

"It is no secret that this is a rich man's club." Putnam's tone turned very frosty.

"But within its hallowed walls, neither business nor politics is ever discussed," I said sarcastically. "Is that it?"

"Exactly."

"Then why are we here?" My smile lacked

sincerity. "Isn't it to talk business about the Whittier Stonewalls?"

"A philanthropic enterprise. I told you that over the telephone, Mr. Victor. I will concede that the members of the Baroquian Club frequently discuss such charities among themselves during their visits here."

I eyed the Secretary of Defense and the munitions contractor, the oil company board chairman and the State Attorney General, the Senator and the building contractor. "I can see that must be it," I agreed.

"And we should get down to our own discussion." Putnam ignored the irony.

"Concerning the Whittier Stonewalls."

"Of course."

"Which the Baroquian Club financed to have enfranchised as a tribute to—"

"No, no, Mr. Victor!" Putnam interrupted me. "The Baroquian Club did no such thing. It has no official connection with the Whittier Stonewalls whatsoever. A few gentlemen met in private to arrange this matter. Believe me, the meeting was quite informal."

"But it took place here?"

"Well, yes."

"And the gentlemen involved are all members?"

"Yes." Putnam's sigh was painful, the sound made by a parent hearing for the hundredth time the query "Why, Daddy?"

"But that's mere coincidence," I summed up for him.

"You may think what you like, Mr. Victor." Putnam reacted to my tone. "But I would ask you to restrain your cynicism when we meet with the other gentlemen concerned with this matter."

"Why should I do that?" I felt like being difficult.

"There are certain proprieties to be observed," his parent informed my child.

"Nuts to the proprieties!"

"If you do not behave, Mr. Victor, your services may have to be dispensed with. I would really regret that."

"Dispense away!" I waved a hand airily.

"So, too, would the services of Mr. Dubrowski."

I looked at Rhino. His basset hound eyes said he needed the job.

"Okay." I owed Rhino. "I'll behave."

"Then, if you're finished with your drinks, gentlemen, I suggest we join my associates in the conference room."

" 'Associates'? 'Conference room'? How unbusinesslike can you get?"

"Mr. Victor—!"

"Sorry. Sorry. It won't happen again." I stood up and fell in with Rhino to follow Putnam from the library.

En route we passed another former President of the United States. "Charles!" He stopped Putnam by stepping directly in front of him. "Ah want yew to know Ah tol' Mama not to let Billy play with them Libyans!"

"I'm sure you did, Mr. President." Putnam's tone was soothing.

"Billy ought to of known not to do his own

brother thataway!"

"He certainly should have, Mr. President."

"An' that business with the Shah, Charles. Why, that was jus' plain ol' Southern hospitality!"

"Of course it was, Mr. President."

"An' David an' Henry an' that Helms fella, why, they all said how he did for us an' so now we had to do for him. Why, hell, what could be more bipartisan than that?"

"You're absolutely right, Mr. President."

"Also, Ah'm a good daddy, Charles. An' a good daddy, he talks about current events with his little girl. An' he listens serious to what she has to say."

"That is most certainly what a good parent should do, Mr. President."

"Then answer me somethin', Charles. Jus' how come Ah'm not the President of these here United States anymore?"

"*Vox populi*, Mr. President. Public ingratitude."

"The people didn't 'preciate me, Charles."

"Indeed not, sir."

"They'll be sorry, Charles. Look what they got. Aged ham! They'll be wishin' Ah was back!"

"They already do, Mr. President."

"Amen!" I echoed, all politicians being relative. We continued on our way. Putnam ushered us into a small, comfortable room with a round oak table surrounded by well-padded chairs. There was also an oak sideboard, glowing with the inevitable brandy and snifters. A cloud of cigar smoke rich as OPEC hung over the room.

There were four men already seated around the table when we entered. One, as conservatively dressed as Putnam, although his grey suit had a muted pinstripe, sported a belly as rotund as a bank vault, along with a moustache which had shaped itself like feline whiskers. A fat cat!

Beside him was a ruddy-faced man wearing plus-fours and a golfer's tam. He was chatting with a small, trim, square-jawed man meticulously clad in the uniform of a three-star General of the Army of the United States. The fourth man, in Arab robes and burnoose, sat with his fingers folded in an arrangement that might have been prayer or might have indicated that his mind was occupied with calculating a per-barrel price raise in keeping with the latest equipment depreciation allowance granted American competitors.

Putnam identified us to this group without introducing any of them by name. "Are we all here?" he wondered.

"Except for the Governor," Fat Cat told him. "He had a rehearsal, but it should be over."

"Here he is now," the Golfer said as the door which Putnam had shut opened and closed again.

I recognized the man who entered immediately. Besides being the governor of a Southwestern state, he was one of the shakers and movers of the Republican Party. His power was so consolidated that few decisions in the areas of energy, military appropriations, or highway subsidies were taken at the national level without a representative of the President's consulting with him first. He was wearing a body stocking with a tutu and angel wings. His legs were shaven. The Governor had really shapely legs.

"Sorry, gentlemen. I didn't have time to change," he greeted us.

"Perfectly all right, Governor," the General assured him. "How's the show going, anyway?"

"It would be going a lot better if Caspar didn't have two left feet. If he runs the Defense Department the way he performs entrechats, the country's in serious trouble. He's throwing off the whole chorus line in the wood nymph number." He crossed his legs, flashing high thigh under the tutu, and lit a cigar. "Did I miss anything?" he inquired.

"No, Governor. We were just about to begin," Putnam told him.

"Now, gentlemen, as I understand it—" Fat Cat, a take-over type, led off the discussion. "—our new scout here, Mr. Duworski—"

"Dubrowski," Rhino corrected.

"Sorry. Mr. Dubinsky here has found us a quarterback. That right, Mr. Balinsky?"

"Dubrowski."

"Whatever." Fat Cat was annoyed. If people didn't like the way you pronounced their name, why didn't they go back where they came from? "But you have found us a quarterback, haven't you, Mr. Kaminsky?"

"Dubrowski," Rhino muttered to himself. "Yes sir, I have. And I can tell you that Terry Niemath has more potential than any new quarterback I've seen in years."

"Terry Niemath!" the golfer exclaimed. "I like that name! It has a lot of promise!"

"Sounds like a serious, God-fearing fellow," the General agreed. "Prayer breakfasts and all that. Is he born again like that other Terry? What's his name?"

"Bradshaw, sir," Rhino told him. "No, Terry Niemath's not born again. As a matter of fact, Terry Niemath's not—"

"More the fun-loving, flashy type, like Joe Namath," the golfer supposed. "Well, we can live with that. It's good box office."

"I hope he doesn't have Joe's weak knees," the Governor worried, plumping up the stuffing in the brassiere he was wearing under his body stocking. (I wondered if he'd snitched it from his sister.) "And I hope he doesn't chase skirts like Joe always did."

"The knees are fine," Rhino assured him. "And there's no problem with girls. The problem is—"

"Yes, tell us," Fat Cat interrupted. "Some sort of sex problem, isn't it? Isn't that why we hired Mr. Vector here?"

"Victor!" I snarled.

"Umm, yeah. The problem ..." Rhino shot me a pleading look.

I shook my head slightly, but firmly. There was no way we could pass Terry off as a man with this bunch. "Tell them," I told Rhino.

"Terry Niemath is a chick!" Rhino blurted out.

"I beg your pardon?" The confusion on Putnam's face spelled out poultry.

"He means a girl, a woman," I explained.

There was a stunned silence while the all-male members of the all-male Baroquian Club raised their eyebrows at one another. The Governor lowered his eyes and contemplated his fingernail polish. The Arab, who had not spoken before, broke the silence now.

"A female quarterback," he said in perfect English, "is against the teachings of Allah, the laws of nature, and the rules of professional football."

"That about sums it up, Mr. Dumasski!" Fat Cat's tone was nasty. "What the hell are we supposed to do with a woman quarterback anyway?"

"There's nothing in the official rulebook against it," Rhino told him. "I looked it up." He took a deep breath. "I wouldn't know about Allah, or nature," he added. It was obvious that he figured he was going to be fired anyway. "And the name is Dubrowski. That's spelled D-u-b-r-o-w-s-k-i. Pronounced Dubrowski. I get real hostile when motherfornicators like you coitus it up!"

"What was that last?" The golfer cupped a hand to his ear.

"He called him a mother-fucker for fucking up his name," the Governor explained.

"Oh, Grace, I just love it when you talk dirty!" The General pinched the Governor's left buttock.

"Gentlemen! Gentlemen!" Putnam restored them to order. "We don't have time for frivolity now."

"Nonsense, Charles." The General took exception. "That's what the Baroquian Club is all about. Fun and games. Relaxation. Letting our hair down. After all, we're all Old Boys, and Old Boys will be Old Boys!"

"Nevertheless, General, I must insist that we get back to the matter at hand."

"Who the devil are you, Charles, to insist on

anything?'' The General was piqued.

''A retired government employee who has kept up his files, General.'' Putnam's smile cut his throat. ''Now, may we proceed?''

''Of course, Charles,'' the General muttered. ''Of course.''

''All the same,'' Fat Cat said, ''how can we countenance a female quarterback? We, who belong to a club that not only bars women as members or guests, but won't even let them on the premises as waitresses?''

''That's right,'' the Arab concurred. The Golfer and the Governor nodded their heads in agreement. The General looked to Putnam for a signal.

''On the contrary, gentlemen,'' Putnam told them. ''This may well be a God-given chance to improve the club's image with the public.''

''What the devil do you mean, Charles?'' Fat Cat wanted to know.

''The Baroquian Club has been made to look foolish because of its all-male politics.'' Putnam ticked off his points briskly. ''This reflects badly on us as members. It reflects on all of our members and some guests as well in their areas of expertise. Unwanted publicity revealing our practice of occasionally dressing up as women has made the public doubt our abilities to run our government, deploy our armed forces, distribute our natural resources, manufacture our automobiles, produce our motion pictures, grow our grapes, and so forth. Our image, in short, is quite tarnished. But suppose a group of prominent Baroquian Club members such as we became the driving force behind the gender integration of professional football? Overnight, gentlemen, we would become civil liberties heroes—forward looking, fair-minded, unbiased men of strong conviction! As a group, we would be likened to Branch Rickey introducing Jackie Robinson to professional baseball."

"Is this woman black?" The General was confused.

"No, General. I was just drawing a parallel," Putnam clarified. "And don't forget, gentlemen, that we also get a competent quarterback, something the Whittier Stonewalls badly need."

"I don't understand, Charles." Fat Cat was deliberately slow on the uptake. "If we won't let women in our club, how can we be in favor of letting one play on our professional football team?"

"If we're for democracy, how could we justify putting the Shah on the throne?" Putnam responded softly.

"If we're against welfare, how can we justify bailing out Chrysler?" the Golfer reminded him.

"If we're for conserving energy, how can we justify the use of electricity to light up outdoor advertising?" the Arab added.

"I see." Fat Cat nodded his head. "Like our humanitarian policies in Vietnam."

"Exactly," the General told him. "Past history, but that's exactly right."

"Then it can be justified."

"Of course," Putnam continued. "More than justified. It will divert attention from our anti stand on the E.R.A."

"Is that still around?" the Golfer wondered.

"I don't think it's going to go away," the Arab told him. "The houris of my harem had a bonfire the other night to burn their veils."

"My wife burned my dinner," the Governor remembered, "when she found out the legislature tabled the vote on the amendment."

"I can see it now." The General looked to Putnam for approval. "The headlines in the papers, I mean. 'Elite Group of Baroquian Club Members Sponsor First Woman Quarterback in Professional Football'!"

"The Right to Organizational Privacy Does Not Mean the Right to Discriminate, Vow Baroquians'!" The Golfer picked up on the theme.

" 'A Woman's Place Is in the Huddle, Not the Baroquian Club, Pro Fem Lib Members Declare'!" Even Fat Cat became part of the general enthusiasm.

"We will steal the fire away from them!" The Arab's eyes were aglow. "While the activists talk, we Baroquians will act!"

"Wait a minute!" Only the Governor had reservations. He smoothed his body stocking nervously over his padded bosom. "Last year, we invited the team to our annual show. Does this mean this quarterback will be invited this year? I mean, I wouldn't feel comfortable doing my wood nymph erotic dance with some woman watching! Besides, it wouldn't be right for a lady to hear all those dirty jokes on the program."

I thought of Terry Niemath and swallowed a laugh.

"Miss Niemath will not be invited to the show,"

100

Charles Putnam reassured him. "Mr. Dubrowski will see to that. Won't you, Mr. Dubrowski?"

"Sure. But there's one other thing that ought to be—"

"And you'll take care of all the other details, won't you, Mr. Dubrowski?"

"Well, yeah. But I'm trying to tell you there's another—"

"Then it's all settled." Putnam stood up. "And since we have other matters to discuss, I wonder if Mr. Dubrowski and Mr. Victor would mind excusing themselves now?"

"You're not listening, Mr. Putnam," I told him. "Rhino here is trying to tell you something. He's trying to tell you there's another problem. Another *sex* problem."

"Another sex problem?" Putnam sat down. "Explain, please, Mr. Victor."

"Our lady quarterback has an over-developed libido," I told him succinctly.

"You mean—?"

"She's a nymphomaniac," Rhino defined, not having to worry about what Stephanie Greenwillow might think.

"Insatiable," I confirmed.

There was a long silence broken by the Arab and the General, speaking together. "Allah save us!" said the Arab. "Oh, shit!" said the General.

"I don't see where her private life need concern us." Fat Cat was calmer.

"If we're worried about our image," pointed out the Governor, biting his knuckle and smearing his lipstick, "it sure as diddly-poo has to concern us."

"Couldn't we get one of our Moral Majority preachers to have a talk with her and make her see that virtue is its own reward?" suggested the Golfer.

"I don't think that would work," I told him.

"I've got it!" The General sprang to his feet. "We'll have her spayed!"

"I don't think she'll go for that either," was my opinion.

"Why not?" The General pounded a fist into the palm of his other hand excitedly. "I once had this bulldog bitch, horniest critter you ever saw, and we took her to the vet and, after he altered her, she was chaste as Maggie Thatcher."

"I don't think she'll go for it." He obviously hadn't heard me the first time.

"Hell, we didn't *ask* this bulldog bitch! We just hauled her on down to the vet and *did* it!"

"I wouldn't suggest you try that, General." Rhino spoke up. "This female canine is one tough football player."

"What do you suggest, Mr. Victor?" It was Putnam who spoke, but now all eyes turned to me, the Man from O.R.G.Y., the sex expert.

"Somebody will just have to ride herd on her every minute of the day and night. Otherwise, the papers will get hold of it, and you gentlemen will look more foolish than you do because of the waitress brouhaha."

"Would you be willing to take on that job for us, Mr. Victor?"

"Hell, no!"

"We sure would be appreciative, Mr. Victor."

102

The Governor batted his false eyelashes at me.

"And generous too, Mr. Factor," Fat Cat added.

"Victor!"

"Very generous." The Arab's eyes measured my weakness. "Doesn't that interest you?"

Chivas Regal ... beautiful women ... lots of money ... these are a few of my favorite things. "Yeah," I surrendered. "It interests me."

"It will not be a problem." Charles Putnam brought the discussion to a close. "We will work out the details between us later, Mr. Victor, and then you and Mr. Dubrowski and Ms. Niemath can proceed to Whittier to join the team. Will that be satisfactory?"

It would be. Rhino and I were eased smoothly from the room and entrusted to another formally dressed butler whose job it was, I presume, to be sure we left the premises. As we went out the front door, I glanced back over my shoulder.

Two middle-aged men in Shirley Temple dance outfits stood licking giant lollipops. "Dig those hoofers." Rhino had also spotted them.

"Hoovers, not hoofers," I told him. "One of those guys is top ranking FBI, and the other's a CIA bigwig."

"That kind of excretion going down sort of makes me curious," Rhino remarked.

"Curious? Curious about what?"

"Well," he answered, "I wonder who's Kissinger now?"

CHAPTER SIX

The first challenge of my new job presented itself sooner than I expected. Terry Niemath, Rhino, and I had taken a night flight from San Francisco to Los Angeles. Another rental car, this one a Porsche (why, I wondered, did Charles Putnam always lean towards German products?), was waiting for us at the airport. I drove it thirteen miles east to the slopes of the Puente Hills, where the expanding city of Whittier once nestled but now sprawls.

Whittier was founded in 1887 by Quakers. The Quakers who followed were mostly farmers, and so Whittier became a farming community. World War II changed both the pacifist solidarity of the area and its bucolic ambience. The farms were replaced by factories manufacturing oil well equipment, machine parts and products made of various steel alloys, car radiators, oil burners, chemicals, plastics, cutlery, and parts for commercial and military aircraft. A miniature Pittsburgh of the Far West, Whittier today has grown to a metropolis of over three hundred thousand people.

I drove through it towards the northwest section, which is bounded by Ross Hills Memorial Park, one of the largest cemeteries in the United States. Not far from it was the residence hotel where the Whittier Stonewalls were lodged during the training season and during the regular season when they weren't on the road. It was a large, squarish structure on a quiet, tree-lined street near the stadium.

The inside lobby was clean, airy and unpretentious. It was after midnight, and the desk clerk was sleepy but polite. He didn't chew gum—always the mark of a class hostel. He was expecting us and had our room assignments and keys ready.

Rhino and I were sharing room 310. Terry was in room 318, down the hall. Naturally, I assumed that hers was a private room, and that she'd be alone in it.

Lesson One for the Organization for the Rational Guidance of Youth: *Never assume!*

The obliging desk clerk helped us up with our baggage. We stopped at Terry's door first. He opened it and handed her the key. Before she could enter, a light went on inside and the doorway was blocked by three hundred plus pounds of pro football offensive tackle on the hoof.

"Howdy, guys. Been expectin' you." His yawn was high and toothy enough for a dinosaur. "Which one of you's Niemath?" As he spoke, somewhere up in the stratosphere where his head was, his brain sent a message to his eyes, and he opened them. They were blue, and large and wide enough for a quick dip, if you like alpine pools. "Dumb, huh?" He ducked his elephant-sized head at Terry. "Sure can't be you, Ma'am." His bright smile—displaying teeth like those on a brand new harrow—said he'd figured it all out. Terry must be the wife of one of us, and the other must be his new roommate. At the same moment, he realized he'd been standing there in underwear which clearly revealed a genital outline the size of two basketballs and a baseball bat—or so it seemed. Out of courtesy to the wife of a new teammate, he quickly did his best to cover this with hands like coal shovels. Standing there like that, he even dwarfed Rhino which, believe me, isn't something even most other football players can do. "Beggin' your pardon, Missus." He acknowledged his state of undress and started backing away from the door.

"Y'all hold up just a minute, now!" Terry stopped him. "It's Ms."

"Sorry, Ma'am. Guess I ain't up on that new women's libber lingo."

"What I mean, sugah, is that I am Terry Niemath."

"You're funnin' me!" He stared. The effect was like freezing the searchlights at a Hollywood premiere.

"In the flesh!"

"Yes, Ma'am!" There was the kind of enthusiasm in his voice that offensive tackles usually reserve for thick, rare steaks. "I'm Nuke Outlaw." He remembered to introduce himself.

"Listen," I interjected, turning to the room

clerk. "I think there's been some mistake."

"No." He consulted his list. "Terry Niemath rooms with Nuke Outlaw in 318. That's the way the team manager set it up."

"Even so, I think you'd better let us have another room for the lady."

"I don't rightly want another room!" Terry pouted.

"I don't have another room," the clerk told me. "We're all filled up. If you hadn't been with the team I wouldn't have held yours."

"All right then," I said desperately. "Rhino, you room with this gentleman and Terry can room with me."

"My roommate's supposed to be Terry Nicmath." There was just enough of an edge in Nuke Outlaw's voice to remind me that he stood almost two feet taller than Muhammad Ali.

"And my roommate's supposed to be Nuke Outlaw." Terry removed one of his hands from over his groin and took it between both of hers. The effect was like Fay Wray's holding King Kong's paw.

"Rhino—?" I turned to him as my last resort.

His gaze rose from eye-level, which was Nuke Outlaw's chest, to up around the ceiling where it was met by a look of stubborn possessiveness. "I don't think so, Steve." Rhino shook his head with a sigh. "Not even the two of us."

"See y'all in the mornin'." Terry sashayed into the room.

"G'night, guys." Nuke Outlaw closed the door on my nose just as I had decided that duty dictated I should retrieve her.

Duty! Hell, there was more to the first challenge of my new job than Terry Niemath's over-active libido. There was brawn like I still couldn't believe, combined with male horniness focused into the single-minded, gridiron-forged concentration of a right tackle determined to get laid. Duty? I'm loyal but I'm not suicidal. Let Charles Putnam try standing between a seven-foot, three-hundred-pound-plus lineman with a hard-on and a willing woman. Not me. After all, she wasn't even officially a member of the team yet. Technically, my assignment hadn't started. And, if it had, why then, I guess I'd simply caved in to the first challenge. I'm the Man from O.R.G.Y.; a lover, not a fighter.

"Come on, dearie," I told Rhino. "It's time for beddy-bye."

The reason we'd taken a night flight from San Francisco to Los Angeles was that Rhino had thought it important that Terry be in Whittier the next day to meet the new coach. He wasn't new just to us, but to the rest of the team as well, having been hired as the sixth replacement in two years who was supposed to have the moxie to revitalize the team. He'd called a meeting for nine the next morning, and Rhino wanted Terry there, so she'd start even with the rest of the team.

To make sure of her attendance, Rhino and I stopped off at her room to pick her up. Nuke Outlaw was with her. His red eyes were slit like oyster shells protecting their pearls. As they walked down the hall in front of us, Terry's gait reminded me of John Wayne's after a week or two of busting new broncos. The long legs of her blue jeans formed a mobile parentheses.

We drove the Porsche to the stadium. Despite our prodding, Terry and Nuke were so somnambulistic that we were the last to enter the locker room where the meeting was taking place. The other members of the team had their backs to us, and the coach, who was about to speak, merely peered at us through thick glasses and motioned for us to take seats in the rear. Either the glasses weren't thick enough, or Nuke's bulk blocked Terry's femininity from his vision. It couldn't have been any ordinary thing to him to have a woman in his locker room. In any case, since Rhino and I shared a philosophy of never facing today what you can put off until tomorrow, we positioned Terry in a chair behind Nuke where she wouldn't be easily seen. Few coaches, we figured, would take the signing up of a female quarterback in their stride.

The coach rapped for quiet. When he had it, he started speaking. "My name is Newtrokni," he said. "Coach Newtrokni. My first name is none of your fuckin' business. You call me 'Coach' or 'Sir.' I don't like jokes about my name. I don't like jokes about Notre Dame, Pat O'Brien, or the Gipper. Player fines start at fifty green ones for those jokes and go up from there. Same for mispronouncin' my name or puttin' a 'K' on the front of it. Any questions?"

He stood there and waited, as wide as he was tall, but with no more fat on him than a Pamplona bull. His brown eyes had the consistency of constipated turds behind his thick glasses. His jaw stuck out like a sledgehammer. Now he resumed speaking, his voice, as before, sounding like a cattle stampede over a gravel pit.

"No questions. Good. Now, this here is a get-acquainted meeting after which you guys can suit up, and we'll have a scrimmage. I'll have more to say before that, but first I'm gonna have the assistant coach call out your names to make sure you're all here and to see what you look like."

The assistant coach read off the names in a voice like the computer in *2001*. Each player responded by answering with his position—"Right guard," "Center," and so forth. Finally he reached the "O's" on his list.

"Outlaw, Nuke," he called metallically.

"Here. Right tackle."

"Why are you yawning, Outlaw?" Coach Newtrokni demanded. "Are we boring you?"

"No, sir." Nuke was sheepish. "I just didn't get much sleep last night."

"That's no excuse, Outlaw. Too much sleep is bad for you. I don't believe in sleep. I like my boys to keep active. You keep active, Outlaw, and you won't be yawning when you shouldn't."

"Yes, Coach." Nuke's jaw muscles worked like tractor valves to suppress another yawn.

"Niemath, Terry." The calling of names continued.

"Here," Terry answered in her fluty feminine voice from behind Nuke Outlaw's heft. "Quarterback."

"You got a cold, or what, Niemath?" Coach Newtrokni demanded.

"No, Coach." The flutiness was more muffled now, as Rhino and I shifted in towards Nuke Outlaw to block her further from view.

"Quarterback..." Coach Newtrokni mused. "Make a note to ask the Doc, can he do something about that voice box," he told the second assistant coach. "Else, how they gonna hear him call the signals?"

The assistant coach completed the roll call. Coach Newtrokni elbowed him aside and again faced the team, rocking from side to side on thick bandy legs. There was open hostility in the gravel being kicked up as he resumed speaking.

"Cards on the table!" he proclaimed. "The Whittier Stonewalls are to pro football what President Ronald Reagan is to the art of summit diplomacy, which is another way of saying this team is a total disaster. Hold it!" His snarl silenced the murmur of protest. "I know most of you guys weren't here the last two seasons when the Stonewalls earned this rep. On the other hand, if you were any good, you wouldn't have been signed up by us this year. You'd have been snapped up by some halfway decent team."

"That go for you too, Coach?" a redheaded linebacker with a faceful of freckles like a measles epidemic wisecracked.

"Now hear this, Foley!" The Coach's voice sank to a hiss like bubbling lava. "I don't like honesty. I don't like forthrightness. I don't believe my players should tell it like it is. I place a high value on humility, kowtowing, and groveling. My good graces are best entered by a regular tugging of the

111

forelock. In short, Foley—and you'd better remember this—my ass is here to be kissed. Any questions?"

"No, sir, Coach. Foley's face had turned so white that it looked like the freckles were dribbling off it.

"The first time any of you forget that could cost you fifty; the second time, a hundred; and the third time, you'll be long gone. Now, to get back to what I was saying about the team. The way I look at it, you guys are a batch of mixed turds, an' I'm the guy with the shovel who has to mold you into a solid shitpile. Practice and training will do that on the field. Discipline will back that up off the field. Now, you'll find I don't operate like other coaches. But the one thing I do have in common with them is that I expect absolute subservience and obedience as regards the rules I set down when it comes to training. These rules have to do with your physical well-being and with your morale."

"Excuse me, Coach Newtrokni." A defensive linebacker named Simon Sabbath held up his hand respectfully. "But I'm sure you want to keep our spiritual well-being in mind, as well."

Lesson One for Defensive Linebackers: *Never assume!*

"Negative!" The Coach didn't actually breathe fire it just seemed like he did. "Now hear this! I am an atheist! I will tolerate no Bible-thumpers on my team! All crosses, mezuzzahs, plastic Jesuses, Buddhas, and other religious artifacts will be turned in to the assistant coach here. There will be no prayer breakfasts! There will be no praying at all! Any player who breaks training by sneaking off to church to pray will be fined. There is no place on my team for born again sinners, Catholics who confess, Jews who observe the High Holy Days, dunked Baptists, Buddhists on the track of Nirvana, transcendental meditators, or any other religious believers of any sort. And, since we are a team, I expect you all to feel the same reverence for atheism that I do. Questions?"

"Beg pardon, Coach." A halfback who had made a name for himself at Columbia dared interrupt. "I'm an agnostic. Is that okay?"

"Negative! Resolve your doubts, Luther. There are no maybes. You want to backslide, you pray I don't find out about it. And you pray to me, 'cause I'm all there is! Your only deity! Anything else is heresy. Questions?"

The room was silent.

"Okay. Now Training Rule One is, no religion. And Training Rule Two is—" He snapped his fingers at the first assistant coach.

"Curfew." The f.a.c. came in on cue smoothly, as if someone had pressed his response button.

"Right. Curfew. There will be no curfew for my team. I want my players to stay out late and get up early. Sleep dulls the senses, and I want my players sharp. All work and no play makes Jack a dull boy. No curfew! No catnaps. No lying around in bed when you could be out cavorting. Now, what do I mean by cavorting?" He snapped his fingers again, this time at the second assistant coach.

"Women!" The s.a.c. spit out the word the way a Salvadoran says "Yankee!"

"Right. Now, some misguided coaches feel that

113

their players should stay away from women and conserve their bodily fluids. I know better. The disposal of semen by use of the orifices of willing women is the best outlet there is for cleansing the body of distracting fluids. It relieves the pressures of desire and frees the body for the business of football. It keeps the whole thing out of the locker room and away from our training quarters. So, go out every night and screw your asses off, fellows. And come back every morning with clear heads and cleansed bodies and play football.''

Simon Sabbath looked on the verge of tears. First he'd been deprived of his religion, and now he was being ordered to sin. What next?''

''What next?'' Coach Newtrokni snapped his fingers at the f.a.c.

''Diet!'' The word whirred from the lips of the f.a.c.

''Right. Diet. Now you men should know that the cornerstone of my atheism is vegetarianism. Some atheists are not vegetarians, and some vegetarians are not atheists, but those poor souls are misguided and could certainly never run a professional football team. Understand me. There will be no steaks at my training table. There will be no red meat. There will be no eggs, milk, or other dairy products.''

''What will there be, Coach?'' a tight end was brave enough to ask.

''Carrot salad. Alfalfa with wheat germ. Zucchini. Raw coconut. Sunflower seeds.''

''Potatoes?'' another player inquired desperately.

"Yams. Mashed, with yogurt. Other health foods, as well. This will build you up and give you the strength to devastate all those lead-bellied meat-eaters you're going to come up against."

"But won't a diet like that leave us hungry, Coach?"

"Of course it will! That's the whole idea. Nobody ever felt satisfied after a meal of raw beets and bean sprouts. You'll be so hungry you'll be savage. You'll be unsatisfied carnivores. You'll tear into that opposing line like a starving pack of jungle cats tear into fresh-killed springbok carrion!"

"Kill!" The s.a.c. snarled.

"Kill!" The f.a.c. gnashed teeth like computer gears.

"Excuse me, Coach. But do we have to drink carrot juice and squeezed celery and like that?"

"Negative! You get to drink—" The finger snap again.

"Beer!" The s.a.c. beat the f.a.c. to the punch.

Lesson One for Second Assistant Coaches: *Never assume!*

"Wrong!" The brown turds behind the thick glasses condemned the s.a.c. "Beer bloats! Hard liquor is much better for you. Hard liquor and stout, which has body. As of right now, bourbon and stout is the official drink of the Whittier Stonewalls! Any objections?"

There were no objections.

"I like to see my men plastered. Plastered is relaxed. Come home sober, and you'll play like a deacon the next day. Come home relaxed and you'll be loose as a goose."

"How about smoking, Coach?" someone inquired.

"Develops the lungs. I recommend a minimum of three packs a day if you want to last on this team."

"Grass, Coach?"

"Stoned is even more relaxed than plastered. I suggest a joint at the start of each game and another one at halftime. Any more questions?"

There were no more questions.

"Okay. Now, just one more thing." The harsh tone changed, softened, became more conciliatory, more paternal. "There'll come a time for each of you when you have a problem that you want to talk over. Maybe it'll be a problem having to do with the team. Maybe it'll be financial. Maybe it'll be personal. Maybe it'll involve a girlfriend, or a sick mother, or a faithful old dog that's dying. Now, guys, do you know who you can go to when you have some such problem?"

Their trusting faces said they knew.

"Coach Newtrokni." The f.a.c. issued the answer.

Lesson One for First Assistant Coaches: *Never assume!*

The Coach ignored him and kept looking at the players. "Well, I hope you know who you can go to when you have some such problem, men. I hope you know, because you sure as shit can't come to me! I don't want to know about your fuckin' problems! Keep 'em to yourself! I'm a coach, not a fuckin' sky-pilot! And don't you guys ever forget it. Now suit up and be out on the field in five minutes. Hop to it, you batch of uncoordinated turds!"

Rhino and I held a quick meeting with Terry behind the bulk provided by Nuke Outlaw. We reached a quick decision. Neither Rhino nor I felt up to facing Coach Newtrokni with the news that one of his new quarterbacks had an empty space where his macho was supposed to be hanging. Rhino summed up our cowardice:

"Let's let Coach get a look at Terry in action before we spring it on him. After he's seen her, he won't mind so much. Believe me."

I didn't believe him, but I was for anything that would postpone the moment of truth. "You don't think maybe he'll notice when she comes out on the field?"

"With a loose jersey, shoulder pads, and her hair under a helmet, she'll get by."

That's what I liked about Rhino. Once he got his teeth into an idea, he never gave up. He was still hoping we could pass Terry off as a guy. It was the kind of sticktoitiveness that had made him a good Marine, the quality that had propelled him to save my life in 'Nam, the trait that would probably get all three of us fired by Coach Newtrokni.

Nuke sneaked the uniform and helmet out of the locker room for us. We found a deserted hallway and Terry dressed there. Rhino and I stood guard at either end of the corridor.

Actually, it wasn't too bad. Terry really didn't look particularly female in the loose-fitting uniform. Rhino added some padding here and there that served to square off her curves. When he was through she looked like a tall candidate for a junior high school team.

We were late getting onto the field. The rest of the team was there already. Coach Newtrokni noticed. "That's fifty, Niemath," he announced. "Late for practice!"

Terry started to protest, but Rhino clapped his hand over her mouth and led her away. He sat her down on the bench with some other players and parked himself between them and her. I hustled over and sat on her other side. We didn't want any premature revelation.

The coach was testing out the candidates for the offensive and defensive lines. He'd set up a four-man standard defense against a five-man split offensive. He kept changing the players, but not the pattern. He wasn't interested in plays. He was trying to gauge speed and muscle and knowhow.

The linemen as a group were short on all three. They looked hefty enough but, when they slammed into one another, you could see there was a lot more grunt than brawn. They were as light on their feet as a bunch of sea tortoises, and their reflexes were strictly slow-motion. Their instincts, on the other hand, guided them as jerkily as Keystone Cops.

I paid particular attention to the offense. These were the guys who'd have to block for our underweight female quarterback if Terry made the team. In pro football, that meant that more than her success in any given game would depend on them. There would be many, many times when her life would depend on them. At her weight, being sacked could definitely be fatal.

Nuke Outlaw was decidedly the size lineman Terry would need for protection. The three of us watched him hopefully as he towered over the opposition when they lined up. When the ball was snapped, Nuke moved surely to the left and took out his own guard and center. The defensive line gratefully paraded through the hole at right tackle. If there had been a quarterback there, the poor patsy would have gone down under more than a thousand pounds of hard-charging and ferocious tacklers. If that quarterback had been Terry, they'd have needed a magnifying glass to find all her pieces and a blotter to pick them up.

Coach Newtrokni was pacing back and forth on the sidelines. As Nuke took out the right half of his own line, he paused in front of us to make a note on his clipboard. I peered over his shoulder, curious to see what it was. Next to Nuke's name, he'd scrawled, "heft plus zilch." A quick glance showed me that Nuke wasn't alone. Next to the names of the other linemen there were similarly derogatory comments.

He started shuffling the linemen around. He tried out the first of the candidates for quarterback with them. With Nuke again blocking away from the play, the poor guy was creamed in the pocket on his first pass attempt. On the second play he tried to run. Coach was writing even before they hit him: "Lollypop legs" was his judgment. From the crazy angles they were pointing at when they carried him off the field, that sounded right to me.

The second candidate handed off three times running to a teammate who wasn't there. The fourth time, he handed off to the defensive guard who—typically—ran the wrong way to score a touchdown for the other side. The quarterback looked pleased with himself at how well things had worked out—almost as if he'd convinced himself he'd planned it that way—and trotted off the field. But then, he hadn't seen Coach's comment: "Puts on pants over head!"

Coach Newtrokni decided to test the third quarterback candidate's passing ability. He stationed a receiver twenty yards away in the right-hand corner. The quarterback underthrew him by ten yards and was at least twenty degrees to the left. After he'd repeated this a dozen or so times, Coach sent him to the showers. The comment was: "Dependable as a *Pinto*."

"Niemath! Get your ass out there! Let's see what you can do! Let's see your arm. How far can it go?"

"Try forty yards," Rhino suggested.

Coach deigned to notice his presence for the first time. "Who the hell are you?"

"Rhino Dubrowski. The scout who signed Niemath."

"You sign those other clunkers?"

"No, sir."

"Well, I guess that's a plus. Let's see what your boy can do."

Rhino winced at the word 'boy' and then yelled to Terry. "Forty-yard pass."

A hopeless receiver jogged forty yards to the ten yard line and stood there with his hands dangling at his side. Obviously he didn't expect the pass to come anywhere near him. A moment later the football bounced hard off his gut, knocking the wind out of him. We could hear him go "Oof!" from the sidelines.

Coach Newtrokni's eyebrows reached for his receding hairline. "Again," he decided.

Terry threw a dozen more passes in a row. The Coach had receivers criss-crossing the field like roadrunners to test Terry's accuracy. She never missed. The receiver didn't always make it, but the ball was always exactly where it was supposed to be when it was supposed to be.

Coach penciled in a comment with my chin on his shoulder. "Arm super; heft puny." Compared to the other comments on his sheet, it was exorbitant praise. "Try a handoff," he ordered Terry.

She handed off so smoothly that the opposing linemen didn't even bother tackling her. She repeated this five or six times. On two of the plays, the running back fumbled the ball and Terry smoothly slipped a hand under it and bobbled it back up into his gut again. A couple of times, the defensive guards broke through in time to break up the play but, in each case, Terry reversed smoothly, avoided them, and managed to hand the ball to the running back so that he caught the tackle instead of her.

The Coach wrote another comment: "Elbow smooth; heft puny." Then he told Terry he wanted to see some fakes. She performed them so well that, even though I knew they were coming, I'd have sworn she handed off the ball when she kept it. Three times running, the defense hit the wrong man and left Terry out in the clear.

The Coach's comment was "Neat magic act, heft puny." He scratched his head and stared out across the field at Terry, who was waiting for further in-

structions. "How are Niemath's legs?" h.
wondered aloud.

"Like you wouldn't believe, Coach," Nuk.
Outlaw told him, remembering.

Coach ignored the comment. "Get out there and
tell Niemath I want to see him break out of the
pocket and run," he instructed Nuke.

Nuke trotted out onto the field and relayed the
message. Terry nodded towards us to show she
understood. It wouldn't have mattered if she
hadn't. With Nuke invariably pulling her pass protection the wrong way, she had no choice but to
run, anyway.

She was fast, really fast. More important than
that, she had a sure instinct when it came to making her moves. She reacted the instant a tackler
committed himself and her reverses and side-slips
were smooth as whipped cream cheese. She
suckered one man after another—sometimes two at
once—and was always somewhere else as they came
up empty.

"Fast feet," the Coach noted. "Heft puny." He
called over a defensive linebacker and conferred
with him. He clued him in on the next play and sent
him in. "I wanna see how that puny little guy
stands up when he's really hit," he confided to
nobody in particular. "This time when he gets
going he's gonna walk into a brick wall."

That's just what it must have looked like from
Terry's vantage point. Her defense folded to the
left and the entire four-man defensive line reached
for her as one man. A thousand pounds is a low
estimate.

*

Terry faded back in the pocket, which was all she could do. But they were too close. She couldn't run. It was too late to pass. It looked as though Terry Niemath was about to be the victim of her first professional football sack.

But I didn't know Terry. None of us did. Not even Rhino knew her well enough to expect what she did next.

She faded way back very quickly. She tucked the ball snugly against one hip. Then, with her free hand, she yanked up her jersey from the bottom and pushed her naked gourds out into the faces of the charging linemen!

There's an old Tarzan movie where the elephants are charging a helpless safari party when Tarzan swings down from a vine directly into their path, yells, "Kawabanga!" and holds up his hand. The elephants screech to a dead stop as if some cosmic force has hit their brakes. That's the way those tacklers stopped now. Terry's naked jugs were sign language for "Kawabanga!" and they stopped those behemoths right in their tracks. Later Rhino swore to me that one of the defense sprouted an instant erection and pole vaulted through the goal posts just as Terry trotted into the end zone for a touchdown.

I missed that. I was distracted by the Coach. He wasn't writing on his clipboard this time. He made his final comment aloud as follows: "Heft puny; great tits!"

123

CHAPTER SEVEN

Immediately after the scrimmage, Rhino and I met with Coach Newtrokni in his private office. "You didn't tell me Niemath had tits." He wagged a finger at Rhino coyly.

"Sorry, Coach."

"I mean, that's the kind of pertinent information a coach has the right to expect a scout to provide, wouldn't you say?"

"Yeah, Coach."

"I read the report you submitted when Niemath signed up and you mentioned a good arm and smooth handoffs and fakes and excellent play-calling and great inside and outside moves, but you never once mentioned that Niemath had tits. Was there some reason you withheld that information, Dubrowski?"

"No, sir," Rhino replied miserably.

"Oh, I think there was. I think that you thought

if I knew about those tits my suspicions would be aroused. Isn't that right, Dubrowski?"

"I don't quite follow you, Coach."

"I think you thought, if I saw those tits, I just might begin to suspect that maybe—just maybe Niemath might not be of the masculine gender."

"Masculine gender?" Rhino was slow on the up-take.

"I think you thought I might suspect Niemath of being a woman. Now, tell the truth, Dubrowski. Isn't that so?"

"Yeah, Coach." Rhino's misery deepened.

"Well, Dubrowski, you would have been right. If I'd known about Niemath's tits, I would have suspected Niemath of being a woman not of the masculine gender. Yep! I most certainly would have!"

"That makes sense, Coach."

"I'll bet you thought I wouldn't like the idea of your signing up a female quarterback for the team, Dubrowski. That right?"

"It crossed my mind, Coach," Rhino admitted.

"Well, you were wrong. Flat-out wrong. To tell the truth, I kinda like the idea of going down in the record books as the coach of the first team to sign up a woman to play professional football. Women are a force in this country today, Dubrowski. I don't at all mind scoring points with them. But do you know what I do mind, Dubrowski?"

"What, Coach?"

"I mind being lied to—even if the lie is just leaving something out. Now, a woman quarterback is gonna give me problems. I shoulda known about them from the start."

"I was gonna tell you, Coach. I was just sort of waiting for an opportune moment."

"Is there anything else you're waiting for an opportune moment to tell me, Dubrowski? Because, if there is, I'm telling you that right now is an opportune moment."

Rhino gulped hard. "Terry likes coitus," he said in a very low voice.

"So?" Coach Newtrokni wasn't too concerned. "I think sex is a healthy outlet for my players. I thought I made that clear this morning."

"It's sort of a little more than likes, Coach. Obsessed, I guess, is more like it. I mean, she wants to have sex all the time. She never stops."

"Well, of course, I wouldn't want her disrupting the team."

"That's the problem, Coach. The way Terry goes at it, it could disrupt the team."

"My luck!" The Coach was bitter. "I finally get a quarterback with really strong potential and there has to be some goddam picayune problem to spoil it."

"It's not picayune." I spoke up for the first time. "It could be major."

"I've been wondering who the hell you are." Coach Newtrokni stared at me suspiciously.

Rhino introduced me and explained about my O.R.G.Y. expertise. "Steve's job is to keep Terry in line and deal with any problems come up 'cause she's a nymphomaniac woman," he summed up.

"Can you do that, Victor?" There was a decided lack of faith in Coach Newtrokni's voice.

"With God's help." I was being ironic.

"You believe in God?" Coach Newtrokni was shocked.

"Somebody must make the subways run on time."

"The subways don't run on time."

"Yeah, I know."

"I don't want to hear about any deities, Victor. I need a quarterback I can depend on. Now, can you—?" He interrupted himself and looked up annoyed as the f.a.c. entered. "What is it?"

"Responding your request immediate injury reports first scrimmage, Coach." His computer voice announced the data output.

"Oh, yeah. Let's see." Coach studied the printout the f.a.c. handed him. "What the hell is this?" he exploded. "There are six groin injuries from the last lousy play!"

"Result of tacklers ditto blockers erections response to quarterback mammaries, Coach."

"Yeah? So? A hard-on isn't a groin injury that I know of."

"Team medic reports quote injuries due to combination blue balls and stubbing dicks against steel jocks unquote."

"Victor?" The Coach turned to me. "You're supposed to be the expert. I can't afford those kind of injuries. What's going to happen when we play a real game?"

I was saved from having to admit I had no answer when the s.a.c. came flying into the room. "Coach! Coach!" He was very agitated. "Come quick! There's a fuckin' riot in the shower room!"

"What kind of riot?" the Coach wanted to know as we all followed the s.a.c. back towards the shower room.

"A fuckin' riot, Coach. I told you."

It was an accurate description. When we reached the shower room, there was a riot going on as well as some spectacular fucking. Both elements seemed to emanate from a hub which consisted of Terry Niemath, Nuke Outlaw, Luther the halfback, and redheaded linebacker Freck Foley.

Terry was on her hands and knees, her long, tanned, sinuous, naked body all slippery and shiny with soapsuds and drops of water. The way she was crouching, her large breasts with their bright red berry nipples swung athletically while her plump, sculpted, pink-clefted ass stuck up high in the air. Just below it, in her wide-stretched pussy, Nuke Outlaw's donkey-size dong was pushing in and out with a rapid rhythm that threatened to split her luscious body in half.

Luther the halfback and Freck Foley were kneeling in front of Terry and attempting to push both their cocks at once into her wet, greedy, red-lipped mouth. Her tongue was extended full-length to lick the undersides of each of their scrotum sacs in turn. Her expression managed to be ravenous and blissful at the same time.

On either side of Terry there was an unconscious football player. Each of them had a slow-dying erection and a large, purple bruise where his jaw should have been.

As we stood staring in the doorway to the shower

128

room, Nuke let out a bellow, slammed his cock hard all the way into Terry's tight—but oily and clutching—quim, and threw a downward punch that caught Luther flush on the jaw. The halfback toppled like a tree and lay behind the other two downed players as Nuke proclaimed his property deed: "Terry is my girl!"

"Y'all shut up an' keep fuckin'," she told him. "I ain't nobody's *girl!* I'm a woman an' the only one whose woman I am is my own!" She signalled to a waiting player to replace Luther.

"No!" Nuke swung and missed.

"Ooh! Sugah! That felt so good!"

Just beyond the two stiff pricks that Terry was sucking, a pair of guards were slugging it out to be next. Beyond them, other soapy, naked players were arguing and struggling to establish their places in line. There were three or four more unconscious bodies strewn around the shower room. Closest to us, defensive linebacker Simon Sabbath was trying to beat up a weak safety named Bubba Weaver. Although Simon had a good fifty to sixty pounds on Weaver, the weak safety was managing to dodge his punches easily. The reason for this was that Simon was fighting one-handed, his other hand forming a firm protective shield over his groin.

"Grinder!" Coach enlisted the aid of Grinder Meade, a black defensive tackle who was almost as large as Nuke Outlaw. "Help me break this up." Coach was trying to get a handle on the overall situation, and Grinder was closest.

The Coach, the two assistants, and Grinder managed to separate Simon Sabbath and Bubba

Weaver. Both players stood naked and panting as the Coach faced them down. Bubba, dwarfed by Grinder and Simon, had an impressive hard-on.

"I'll kill him!" Simon Sabbath was in tears.

"Why?" the Coach asked.

"He tried to stick his—his—in my—my—"

"He came right over to me and turned around and faced the shower room wall and wagged his ass," Bubba Weaver said. "I was provoked."

"I wanted to get as far as possible from that depravity!" Simon pointed dramatically at Terry licking the two sets of prick-and-balls by turn as she slammed her ass back and forth on Nuke's embedded cock. The look on her face was sheer bliss. "I turned around because I didn't want to look at that Jezebel seducing my poor, flesh-tempted teammates."

"You saying you didn't wiggle your butt at me?" Bubba Weaver demanded.

"I always move like that. Serpentine. Evasive action. I trained myself to do it reflexively."

"Why?" the Coach demanded. "You're a defensive linebacker, Sabbath, not a ball carrier. Why should you be practicing offensive moves?"

"I don't always want to play defense, Coach. I want to better myself."

"Better yourself?"

"What he means, Coach," Grinder explained drily, "is that offense gets paid better—which is probably why most of the brothers get stuck on defense."

The Coach leaned over to Grinder and spoke in a low voice. "You think that one tried to stick his

130

pecker in his bunghole?''

"Sure he did."

"Why?"

"Old Bubba's gay. Everybody knows that. He don't keep it a secret. Waggin' your ass at him like Simon did is just askin' for it.''

We were distracted by the sound of two loud, crunching punches. Nuke was holding his fists up threateningly. In front of Terry's now empty mouth there were two more unconscious bodies with slow-dying erections. "My woman!" Nuke was bellowing as his balls slapped hard against Terry's hot-flushed and quivering ass and he prepared to come.

"Why is that tackle decking all my players?" Coach demanded.

Rhino explained about Terry rooming with Nuke. "Now he thinks she's his property," he concluded.

"I'll put a stop to that!" Coach was firm.

"How?" I was curious.

"Outlaw and Niemath won't room together any more. And, if he insists, I'll suspend him. Don't worry. Outlaw wants to play. He'll fall into line."

"Who is going to room with Terry?" I wondered.

"You're some sex expert, Victor!" the Coach snorted at me. "That's easy. And it solves the problem, too. The question is, why didn't you think of it?"

"Think of what, Coach?"

"Having Terry Niemath and Bubba Weaver room together. He's gay. Gay! Get it, Victor? No lech for women. Gay! Ergo, no problem!"

"Ergo!" I echoed, keeping any doubts I might have had to myself.

131

"Now, let's break up this scene," Coach ordered.

"How?"

"Throw cold water on them."

And that's what he did. He and the two assistants turned on the ice cold water full blast on all the showers. The fights and arguments tapered off. Finally even Terry screamed and achieved her icy orgasm. As she and Nuke finally uncoupled, Coach asked a question. "How did this start?" he demanded.

"It was my fault, Coach," Terry admitted. "Sorry."

"I guessed you provoked it. What I'm asking is how?"

"I dropped the soap." Terry smiled her Cheshire smile. "I dropped the soap and when I bent down to pick it up, the orgy began."

Events moved quickly after that. For one thing, the Whittier Stonewall cheerleaders arrived on the afternoon bus. They were not happy to learn that a member of their sex had been signed as a team quarterback. They went *en masse* to protest to the Coach. "Mr. Steve Victor deals with all matters having to do with sex and so forth," he told them. "See him." So they descended on me.

Their spokesperson was Buffy Smith, a brown-haired girl-next-door type with all-American breasts. "Two-four-six-eight, this we don't appreciate," she informed me. "Boys play football. Girls are cheerleaders. If you let a girl play footbal, then a boy might want to be a cheerleader. What about that?"

"There are lots of male cheerleaders," I reminded her.

"Not on the Whittier Stonewalls cheerleading squad."

"I should think you'd be glad to see a woman open up new horizons."

"We're cheerleaders. We root for the 'Walls. She'll confuse the boys on the team. She'll undermine their morale. She'll interfere with our keeping their spirits up. They won't play as well."

"As well as what? They've lost their last thirty-six games."

"That proves my point. They lost thirty-six games and their morale couldn't have been better. We girls take credit for that."

"How the hell could you keep their morale up when they're 0 for 36?"

"Show him, girls."

They lined up in front of me. Buffy gave a signal. "STRAWBERRY SHORTCAKE, PINEAPPLE PIE! V-I-C-T-O-R-Y! WILL WE WIN ONE? SOON, WE GUESS! WHITTIER! WHITTIER! YES-YES-YES!" They went through their cheerleading motions as smoothly as the Rockettes. And on the final 'YES!' they raised their short white pleated cheerleader skirts all together. I stared. "See what I mean about keeping up morale?" Buffy asked.

"Yeah." I kept staring. "I see." They weren't wearing any panties!

"It keeps our loyal fans coming back, too," she pointed out.

"I'll bet morale isn't all it keeps up."

"Why, thank you, Mr. Victor."

133

"What do you do about the TV cameramen covering the games?" I wondered.

"It gives them a real approach-avoidance conflict. They have to resolve it for themselves."

"Approach-avoidance conflict, hey?" I managed to get my eyes up from the pudenda display to Buffy Smith's face.

"I was a psych major before I dropped out of college to devote myself to the Whittier Stonewalls."

"Why did you do that?"

"Admiration for the man the team honors."

"What the hell could you find to admire about him?"

"What are you, Mr. Victor?" She definitely didn't like the question. "Some kind of rad-lib Commie-pinko or something?"

"Well, I do live in New York," I admitted modestly.

"That figures!"

"Let's get back to your beef. Just what is your concrete objection to Terry Niemath?"

"We're fearful that she might have intercourse with the players."

"Why would she want to do a thing like that?" I inquired innocently.

"You don't know women, Mr. Victor."

Well, that was true. The more I find out, the less I know. But I am the Man from O.R.G.Y., and so I keep on investigating. "You don't want the players to have intercourse with her?" I inquired.

"What do you think cheerleaders are for?"

"I've often wondered," I admitted. "I'll do everything I can to keep Terry from shtupping the

134

players," I promised, to mollify Buffy Smith. "Everything in my power."

"Such as?"

"Well, we're going to have her room with Bubba Weaver."

"He's gay."

"Exactly."

"A step in the right direction. Women are anathema to Bubba." She said it as if she had reason to know. "Still, we'd prefer it if she were dropped from the team."

"We need a competent quarterback. Terry's the best we've got."

"In that case, Mr. Victor, I have a suggestion to make. It may seen extreme, but I want you to promise you'll give it serious consideration."

"I promise. What's the suggestion?"

"Outfit Terry Niemath with a chastity belt, Mr. Victor, and give me the key. Will you do that, Mr. Victor?"

"I'll think about it," I promised.

I was true to my word. I did think about it. *Incredible!* I was still thinking about it one night about a week later when offensive left guard Plowboy Palmer knocked on the door to my room and entered. "Coach said I should see you, Mr. Victor," he announced.

"What about?"

"I got me this sex problem, sorta."

Somehow, Coach Newtrokni had interpreted my function as that of sexual counselor to the entire team. No way had Putnam hired me for that purpose. Nevertheless, in the interests of harmony, I went along with it.

"What kind of sex problem?" I asked Plowboy.

"Ain't no sheep in Whittier." He hung his head unhapily.

"That's true."

"Yes, sir.'

There was a long silence while I waited for him to explain. When he didn't, I repeated the question: "What's your problem, Plowboy?"

Slowly, haltingly, but with agrarian candor, Plowboy spelled it out. He'd grown up on a sheep ranch in Montana. His first sex experience had been with a pet lamb who had innocently performed fellatio on him. His first coitus had involved a full-grown sheep and hip boots. He had not been faithful to his first love. Having once tasted the joys of ovine amour, the adolescent Plowboy had more or less run amok. Before he left to join the team, he balled every ewe on the ranch. "I ain't had a sheep since shearing time," he confessed, "and my balls is turnin' sky blue."

"Have you told any of the other fellows on the team about this?"

"My roommate."

"What did he say?"

"He laughed a lot. You know how them offensive backs is."

"That's all?"

"Well, he did allow as how he thought he might be able to fix me up with a chicken, but he never did come through."

"Plowboy." I had a sudden thought. "Were you in the shower room the day there was all that to-do?"

"No, sir. I was late showin' up for trainin'. Coach fined me. It was worth it, though. I was at the San Diego Zoo lookin' at them horned Barbary critters. They sure 'nuf are sexy."

"Plowboy, you know what you did with those sheep? Well, you could do the very same thing with a woman."

"Gee, Mr. Victor, I don't think so. It's be too hard a-gettin' 'em set up in the hip boots."

"Plowboy, you don't need the hip boots."

"I don't rightly think ladies 'd let me tether 'em to the wall of the stall," he said doubtfully.

"You don't have to tether them, Plowboy."

"Just truss 'em up, hey?"

"Nope, Plowboy. Just climb into bed with them."

"But what holds 'em still?" Plowboy was confused.

"They don't hold completely still. They move around a little. But you'll like that, Plowboy."

"Maybe." He was still dubious. "But what'll keep 'em from jumpin' the corral—I mean the bed?"

"They won't want to do that. Trust me." I had a sudden idea. "You know Buffy Smith, the head cheerleader?" I asked him.

"Sure thing."

"You think she's—umm—attractive?"

"Well, she's no Merino, but she's not bad."

"You invite her out for a beer tonight."

"Okay. Then what?"

"See what develops." From my experience, something was sure to develop. If I was any judge, Buffy Smith was just the lady to guide Plowboy out

137

of the pasture and into the hay.

"Okay." Plowboy got up to leave and turned in the doorway. "But what about sheep, Mr. Victor?" he asked plaintively.

"If it doesn't work out with Buffy," I promised him, "I'll buy you an angora dildo."

My reputation as a solver of sexual problems spread. Each day brought a new dilemma to my doorstep. Football players, it seemed, were just like the rest of us in having trouble getting their erotic shit together.

There was the tight end, Craig Cramp, toilet-trained too early, who had trouble relaxing with a woman because of his fear of making caca in bed. There was Horseshoe Cohen, the field goal kicker, who had difficulty positioning his equipment between the labia of his ladylove. There was defensive lineman Ambrose Pierce—the team's most penalized player for offsides encroachments, and penetrations of the neutral zone—who, whenever he got near an erogenous zone (which he Freudianly called "the erroneous zone"), ejaculated prematurely. There was Hans Brinker the middle linebacker, known for frequently plugging the wrong hole onfield, who was always making the same mistake in the sack. And there was wide receiver Pete Gorgonzola who couldn't sustain a relationship because, whenever he had an orgasm, he picked up the woman in both hands and bounced her on the floor and yelled "TOUCHDOWN!"

I advised Craig Cramp to seek out a playmate

138

who was into water sports. I recommended contact lenses for the field goal kicker on and off the field. I counseled the defensive lineman to memorize the political speeches of Ronald Reagan and to repeat them to himself while making love or waiting for the snap. I enlightened middle linebacker Brinker on the joys of anal sex. And I assured wide receiver Gorgonzola that his compulsion to claim credit by smashing the ball—or the woman—on the ground would be cured just as soon as he actually did score a touchdown.

Time speeds by quickly during the training season. The period was all but over when I received the telephone call from Cindy Lou Marzipan asking me to pay her a visit. Cindy Lou was the wife of offensive team captain Mitch Marzipan, the center. She was the organizer and leader of the Whittier Stonewalls wives' Total Woman movement. An invitation from her was a command.

It was mid-afternoon when she answered my doorbell ring. She was wearing a pink bow in her hair, pink lipstick, pink eye-shadow, a gauzy pink negligee over a pink shortie nightgown, fuzzy pink slippers with pink pompoms, and a wide toothy smile that revealed healthy pink gums. "How nice of you to come, Mr. Victor." She held out a martini to me in one hand and a plate of brownies in the other.

Dripping gin and dropping crumbs, I followed Cindy Lou Marzipan into the livingroom. She was easy to follow. The way her hips and bottom rolled reminded me of making it on a waterbed. Soft.

Basic rhythm. Lots of bounce.

She arranged herself fetchingly on a pink couch with a floral design of pink flowers and indicated that I should also seat myself there. She looked at me intensely. It was probably an illusion, but I could have sworn the pupils of her eyes were star-shaped.

"I wanted to speak with you, Steve—you don't mind if I call you Steve, do you? Good. And you can call me Cindy Lou. Anyway, I wanted to speak with you about this lady quarterback, Miss Terry Niemath."

"All right, Cindy Lou."

"We Whittier wives are worried about this wench," she alliterated.

"You mean because of your husbands, Cindy Lou?"

"Oh, no, Steve. We know our husbands won't stray. We are, after all, Total Women!" She re-arranged the negligee to display a sleek and shaven thigh. "Total!" she stressed.

"I see. Then what is the problem?"

"Appearances, Steve. We are very concerned about the team image. How will it look? One lady and all those big, brawny, lovable men? When they go on the road, for instance. The fans are bound to wonder who she's sleeping with."

"We're taking precautions to see that she isn't sleeping with anybody."

"But she'll have to share a room with somebody on the road."

"It's no problem. We've got her rooming with Bubba Weaver."

"The gay safety? But how clever of you, Steve."

I saw no reason to tell her it had been the Coach's idea. "Then you think Bubba and Terry will manage to keep it platonic?" I asked.

"Oh, yes! Absolutely! Every one of those cheerleaders has tried to seduce Bubba and failed. He lusts for men, and only for men. Confidentially, Steve, a couple of wives—Total Women, mind you!—made themselves available to Bubba. Their fidelity was not even dented. That's how single-mindedly gay he is."

"I thought Total Women never strayed. Particularly pro football wives."

"Ordinarily, we don't. We devote ourselves totally to our husbands—to fulfilling their domestic needs, their erotic needs, and their spiritual needs."

"Coach Newtrokni isn't going to like that last."

"Our strategy is to avoid confrontation with him while continuing to meet our wifely obligations. We would no sooner stop praying for our husbands than we would cease cooking their favorite dishes or anointing and packaging our bodies to attract them."

"But you said these two women almost did stray."

"Strain, Steve. Can you imagine what a strain it's been for us wives to be *Total* for our husbands when they never win a game?"

"Never even score," I sympathized.

"Exactly, Steve. They never score. We drench ourselves in perfume, cook them aphrodisiac meals, pray for the split-second timing to achieve mutual orgasm, and do you know what the result is?"

"What, Cindy Lou?"

"O for 36. That's what, Steve! Is it any wonder that, occasionally, temptation proves too much for us?" She leaned forward pinkly, blinked her five-pointed eyes, and allowed the pink negligee to slip from her bosom to reveal the pink outlines of pink nipples under the extremely thin pink material of her shortie nightie. "Our husbands don't score, Steve. That's our problem. My problem! We Whittier wives are at our wits' end. We simply can't wait any longer for them to score. We need satisfaction now! Now!" Cindy Lou leaned towards me panting, lips moist, generous breasts heaving, thighs flushed. "What should we do, Steve?" Her hand burned on my thigh. "What should *I* do?"

"I don't really think—" Considering my counseling position, it didn't seem a good idea to take on the team captain's *Total* wife.

"Help me, Steve!" Cindy Lou put her arms around me, pressed her soft breasts against my chest, and leaned back with her eyes half-closed and her pink lips parted and waiting to be kissed. "Help me!"

"Listen." I tried to resist. "The first game is just around the corner. With Terry quarterbacking, the team's bound to score. Just be patient, and your husband—"

"I can't be patient." There were tears in her eyes. "I need satisfaction. I need it now." She unzipped my fly and slid to her knees in front of me. "I'm desperate!" Kneeling with her thighs wide apart, she slipped one hand under the shortie nightie. She pushed aside my jockey shorts and pulled my prick out of my pants. "You have to help me, Steve!" She opened her pink, girl-next-door mouth and took the head of my prick between her pink lips. "You have to help me!" she insisted in a muffled voice, speaking around it. "I need you!"

I'm a bleeding heart. I always come through for charity. I can't resist a fellow human being in need.

I came in Cindy Lou Marzipan's mouth.

A few nights later I was awakened by a rhythmic thumping over my head. The room above me was occupied by Terry Niemath and gay safety Bubba Weaver. It way my responsibility to investigate.

When I entered their room, the condition of the quarterback and the weak safety was *in flagrante delicto*, to put it mildly. Naked as uncracked egg-shells, they had just broken the bed with their un-bridled athletic enthusiasm. Terry had her long legs locked around Bubba's neck. Her plump, rosy bottom was vibrating like a Mixmaster. Her volup-tuous breasts were being shaken as ferociously as a bone in the mouth of a terrier. Their nipples stood up like bright red lipsticks.

As for Bubba, his meager ass was a blur of erotic motion. His brandy chest was huffing like a steam engine. And his fully erect cock was plunging in and out of Terry's willing quim with an unques-tionable heterosexual fervor.

Was it possible? Had Terry done the trick? Was it possible that the Whittier Stonewall's gay safety wasn't gay any more?

The following afternoon Terry Niemath played in her first professional football game. Watching her, I started thinking once again about Buffy Smith's suggestion regarding a chastity belt.

CHAPTER EIGHT

"There's only one solution, Victor. You'll have to room with her yourself. Now, get outa here. I've got a gameplan to go over with my offense." Such was Coach Newtrokni's response to the sexual overindulgence of quarterback Terry Niemath when we discussed it shortly before the first game of the season.

The game was being played at home in Whittier's Milhous Stadium before what was anticipated to be a record-breaking underflow crowd of ten thousand. (Capacity was 68,000.) Nor could those who attended be characterized as loyal Stonewall fans. What pulled them out was the prospect of seeing the Pittsburgh Steelers in action—even if the action was expected to be no more than a one-sided scrimmage for Terry Bradshaw and his teammates. There was no such thing as an optimistic Whittier fan. Two scoreless seasons had made cynics of them all.

To pit the Whittier Stonewalls against the Pittsburgh Steelers, cracked one sports columnist, was the most uneven sports contest since the lions chewed up the Christians. There was one difference that the columnist couldn't have known about. The morale of the Christians had been much higher than that of the Stonewalls. Both groups, however, sought mercy by the same means, one which was frowned upon by the Establishment responsible for their plight.

My first inkling of this insofar as the Stonewalls were concerned came when I slipped into the locker room john at Milhous Stadium to take a piss. There, kneeling on the tiles of the lavatory floor, were two members of the secondary and a wide receiver. Standing in front of them and reading from an open Bible was defensive linebacker Simon Sabbath.

"Give us this day our daily bread and forgive us our trespasses, as we forgive those who trespass against us. . . ." I watched unnoticed as he read the entire psalm. When he finished, he bowed his head. "Let us pray together," he suggested. "Dear Lord, please just get us through this day without fatal injury."

"Lead me not into the path of Franco Haiirs, Lord."

"Deliver me from John Stallworth."

"Yea, though I walk in the shadow of Mean Joe Greene, protect my weak ankles, Oh Lord."

"Hear us, O Lord," Simon Sabbath prayed fervently. "Save us, we pray, from the terrible and bone-breaking destructive wrath of the Steeler's offense and from the cruel and merciless crunch of he Pittsburgh defense, as well."

"Jiggers!" Another player stuck his head in the door behind me. "Coach is heading this way!"

Immediately the four praying Stonewlls leaped to their feet and affected casual attitudes. Simon Sabbath hid the Bible under his jersey. One of the secondary defense players lit up a joint and passed it to the other one. The wide receiver began talking in a loud, jocular voice: "...so the farmer's daughter has her feet in the stirrups and the traveling salesman's just getting on top of her when all of a sudden the farmer sticks his pitchfork in the hay and ..."

Coach Newtrokni shouldered through the door, his hands already unzipping his fly as he headed for the urinal. "What are you guys doing here?" he demanded over his shoulder as he started to pee.

"Just relaxing before the game, Coach, like you said we should."

"You sure you didn't sneak in here to pray?"

"Break training right before the game, Coach?" Simon Sabbath replied in an injured voice. "We'd never do a thing like that."

"Well, you'd better not ever let me catch you doing it! Game or no game, I'll bench any player caught so much as folding his hands suspiciously!" He zipped up his fly. "Why are you standing there in the corner like that, Victor?"

"Just meditating." I said the first thing that came into my mind.

"Is that like praying?" Coach Newtrokni had a

suspicious nature.

"Only if you write Zen poetry," I assured him.

"How long you been here?"

I shrugged.

"You see these guys do any praying?"

Half a ton of Stonewalls managed to look at me pleadingly and threateningly at the same time. "Nope. All I saw them do was sniff, shoot up and jerk off." I like to think I wouldn't have finked even if I didn't bruise so easily.

Coach snorted and left the john. The players followed him out. I did what I'd come in to do. While doing it, I reflected. (Nope, Coach, that's not the same as praying.)

Pre-game prayer meetings were common among some pro football teams, most notably the Dallas Cowboys. Such rites usually took the form of praying for victory. Praying for victory was considered to be a way of keeping up morale.

But the Stonewalls who prayed had never mentioned victory. They had prayed only not to be seriously injured. They had no morale to keep up. It was no attitude for players to take into a ball game.

"God help us!" I said aloud. And then I found myself looking around guiltily for fear that the Coach might have heard. Nevertheless, I whispered it again. "God help the Stonewalls!"

Pittsburgh won the toss and chose to receive. Word was that Bradshaw had injured his arm in practice the day before and Swann was playing with a badly sprained ankle. Because of this, the point spread against Whittier only totalled twenty. Still,

148

the bookies couldn't give away the short end.

The rumor about Bradshaw's arm was probably true. He called a running game through most of the first quarter. Pittsburgh scored only one touchdown on an eight yard run straight up the middle by Franco Harris. But the seven-zero first quarter score didn't really tell the story. That was reflected by the respective times of possession which were Pittsburgh twelve minutes forty seconds, Whittier two minutes twenty seconds. During the time they held the ball, the Whittier Stonewalls managed to lose only twenty-seven yards.

Coach Newtrokni chose not to put Terry Niemath in during the first quarter. He was understandably nervous about what the response would be to the league's first lady quarterback. Besides, he was saving her for when things got really bad.

"Really bad" is a matter of definition. When it began to rain quite heavily at the start of the second quarter, it was a break for Whittier rather than for the Steelers, because Pittsburgh continued to maintain its one-sided possession of the ball throughout the period. This meant they had more of a chance to slide around in the mud, take occasional pratfalls, miss passes, and fumble the slippery ball.

Pittsburgh lost possession through fumbles three times in the second quarter. (Whittier lost it back the same way and added three more fumbles all their own.) The ball popped in and out of Stallworth's hands twice on long passes and Lynn Swann fell on his face twice diving for incompletes. Bradshaw's legs slid out from under him in the

149

pocket before he could pass and he managed to do what the Whittier defense hadn't even come close to doing yet—sack himself. He switched back to a running game in which the mud continued to give Pittsburgh more problems than the Stonewalls' secondary. The result was that Pittsburgh scored only one touchdown in the second quarter, so that, going into halftime, we were behind only fourteen-zip. Considering the Stonewalls' history, we were doing fantastically well.

"Don't let it go to your heads," was the kickoff to Coach Newtrokni's locker room pep-talk. "They're a powerful team and they're known for piling up points in the second half. We have to guard the lead."

"Pittsburgh ahead by fourteen, Coach, sir," the f.a.c. reminded him.

"I know that. It's their lead I'm talking about. My strategy is not to let them add to it."

"What about winning, Coach?" the team captain wondered.

"Don't ask for the moon, Marzipan. Not when we have the stars."

"What stars, Coach?" The center was confused.

The Coach merely winked at him and changed the subject. "Now, I want you guys up for the second half," he said, "so, to get our blood boiling, we're going to have a rousing cheer for Ralph Ingersoll, Madeleine Murray, and atheist Americans everywhere."

"Who are they?" Freck Foley whispered to Grinder Meade.

"I think Ingersoll played secondary for the old

150

Chicago Bears," the tackle replied. "I never heard of Murray."

"RAH-RAH-RAH! SIS-BOOM-BAH!" Coach Newtrokni led the cheers. "HERESY! HERESY! RAH-RAH-RAH!"

"YAY!" the team responded. "YAY! YAY! YAY!" and they trotted back onto the field for the second half, mudsliding the last ten yards into position to receive.

Defensive weak safety Bubba Weaver plopped down on the bench beside me to watch the Whittier offense in what passed for action. "How's it going, Bubba?" I asked him, angling my umbrella to share it with him.

"Did you know every man on the Pittsburgh offensive line can bench-press up to five hundred pounds?"

"That bad, huh?"

"You try playing 'bump-and-run' with Webster and Kolb. The way it works out is, I bump, and they run all over me. It's like charging into a steamroller head-on every time. Oh, well," he sighed. "At least it keeps my mind off my problems."

"What problems?" I recalled his enthusiastic heterosexual performance with Terry Niemath the night before. "I thought you solved your main problem."

"And I thought you were supposed to be a sex expert!"

Time out was called on the field. The Whittier quarterback had attempted a sneak and been brought down behind the line of scrimmage by Number Seventy-five, Mean Joe Greene himself.

Now they were digging him out of the mud where Mean Joe had planted him. It took a while.

Finally, they carried the quarterback's unconscious body off the field and past us to the locker room. I expected Coach Newtrokni to put Terry Niemath in to replace him. But, evidently, things weren't bad enough for that yet. He signaled the third string QB onto the field instead.

"I am a sex expert." I responded to Bubba Weaver's comment.

"Then why do you think balling a woman solved my problem?"

"It means you don't have to be gay."

"Being gay was not a problem for me, Mr. Victor. I was happy gay. I was well-adjusted. I cruised. I had variety. And, sometimes, I had satisfying relationships."

"You didn't exactly look like you were suffering last night with Terry," I reminded him.

"I wasn't suffering. I was tempted and I gave in. Just the way some straight guys are tempted into a gay act and give in. But one act doesn't make them gay, and one act for me doesn't make me straight."

"Okay," I granted. "I can appreciate that."

"But it gave me problems. I mean, a little while ago, I caught myself looking at one of the cheerleaders with lust in my heart."

"Like Jimmy Carter."

"What?"

"Nothing. Go on."

"I started noticing breasts and legs and asses. *Women's* breasts and legs and asses!"

"Nice, huh?"

152

"It confuses me."

"Maybe you're bisexual," I suggested.

"Everybody's bisexual. I'm not talking about potential. I'm talking about preference. I'm talking about commitment to what makes me happiest."

"Which is?"

"Guys. Women just mix up my head. I don't need it. I want to be happy again. I want to stay gay!"

"Okay," I shrugged. "Suit yourself."

"I will. But I need help," Bubba Weaver confided. "I need you to tell Coach I shouldn't room with Terry Niemath any more. I can't stand it. I mean, she walks around nude all the time. Tits flying. Ass wiggling. Pussy puckering. It's more than I can stand. I've got to get away from her. Will you help me, Mr. Victor? Will you talk to Coach Newtrokni?"

"Relieve your mind, Bubba," I told him. "It's already done. You can room with Rhino and I'll room with Terry myself." I didn't tell Bubba that the Coach had decided that before the game began. It couldn't hurt for him to think I was doing him a favor. You never could tell when I might want one in return.

By now, the Whittier third-string QB had succeeded in reaching a fourth-and-twenty-seven situation on the Whittier eighteen. Our punter went in and kicked a long one. The mud fouled up the Steelers' punt return, and their offense took over on their own thirty-eight yard line.

"Problem solved," I reminded Bubba as the Whittier defense dragged back onto the field.

"Now get out there and play your heart out."

Three plays later, he tried to stop Franco Harris and was helped off the field reciting a Gay Rights platform in a voice like Woody the Woodpecker's. On the next play, Number Twelve lobbed a long one into the waiting hands of Number Eighty-eight, and the Bradshaw-Swann connection left Pittsburgh with a first-down-goal-to-go situation. On the second attempt, Franco Harris took the handoff straight up the center for the TD. Mike Bahr kicked the extra point.

In possession again, Whittier chewed up time without much to show for it. Although the luck of the mud was on their side and they managed to eke out three consecutive first downs, they still weren't even within field goal-kicking distance of the Pittsburgh goal posts when they were forced to give back the ball.

Coach sent Bubba Weaver back into the game. Two plays later, Bradshaw lobbed a long one towards Stallworth. But dependable old Eighty-two slipped in the mud and the ball went over his head. Bubba, too far back to have covered, nevertheless turned in time to see the ball in the air and took a hopeless dive back towards it. He landed on his back and slid ten yards to where the ball fell into his upstretched hands.

It was ruled a valid interception. Once again, Whittier had possession. Miraculously, they still had it two plays later when the whistle blew ending the third quarter. The score was Pittsburgh twenty-one, Stonewalls zilch, which took care of the point spread.

With the start of the fourth quarter, Coach Newtrokni decided that the situation was severe enough to warrant putting in Terry Niemath at quarterback. On his instructions, the team slogged through the mud to the scrimmage line as a unit. Terry was in the center of them. Her helmet was on, and her loose jersey and certain strategic padding camouflaged her figure. Like Rhino, the Coach figured it was worth a shot at least to try to conceal her womanliness.

Pete Gorgonzola, the wide receiver I'd counseled about sustaining relationships, followed in their wake. As he passed me, I called out to him. "How's it going, Pete?"

"The same."

"This is your chance to change it."

"Huh?"

"Score a touchdown, and I guarantee things will be better."

"Fat chance."

So much for team spirit. I sat back under my umbrella and watched the Whittier Stonewalls line up in the rain. It was third down with seventeen to go on their own twenty-two. Some situation for a quarterback to face in a first professional football appearance.

With the exception of Terry, the team was soaked to the skin and covered with mud. Mean Joe and the rest of the Pittsburgh defense didn't miss that fact. It made this new undersized quarterback easy to watch. Translation: easy to sack.

The fans, drenched and disgusted, were already starting to drift out of Milhous Stadium as the teams lined up for the first play of the fourth quarter. The whistle blew, and center Mitch Marzipan snapped the ball to Terry. She faded back into the slot.

Pete Gorgonzola did his best to break loose and head deep for the left-hand corner. Pittsburgh safety Mike Wagner, however, was with him all the way. He did a bump-and-run number on Gorgonzola that had the wide receiver bouncing around like a basketball being dribbled by the Harlem Globetrotters. The result was that Pete was nowhere near in position when Terry was ready to throw.

Meanwhile, Terry's blocking was dissolving around her. For once, Nuke Outlaw had made the right move and considerably slowed down his side of the line. Plowboy Palmer was also performing yeoman service at left guard, considering that he had to contend with Steve Furness. Nevertheless, the Whittier line, after giving Terry their all, was now being overrun.

Terry reacted smoothly. Fading still further back in the pocket, she waited for Furness to commit himself and then twisted smoothly away from his bulk. She headed for the right side where Mean Joe Greene was waiting, spotted him, and quickly reversed herself. And all the time she was watching Pete Gorgonzola in order to gauge her pass so he'd be where he was supposed to be to catch it.

She faded still further back. Gorgonzola was free of Mike Wagner now, but the timing was way off. The whole defensive line descended on Terry like a wall of brick toppling in an earthquake. Gorgonzola twisted his head, looked for the ball, didn't see it, turned away and threw up his hands to indicate the hopelessness of the situation as he trotted towards the goal line. Terry tossed the pass and back-pedaled away from the tacklers without being touched.

The ball soared through the air. It was a beautiful pass, sixty yards or more. It was heading straight for where Gorgonzola was going to be—in the left-hand corner just beyond the twenty-yard line. But he was making no further effort to catch it. He was still looking in the direction and waving his hands loose-wristed over his head, resigned to failure. Pittsburgh safety Mike Wagner had stopped trying to cover him and was just watching his receding figure and laughing.

At the eighteen-yard corner, the ball fell from the air and right into Gorgonzola's upstretched hands from behind. Automatically, he closed his large palms around it. He stood there for an instant and stared at it.

Upfield Mike Wagner's jaw fell open. He blinked. He muttered what might have been a curse. And then he was off like a shot after Gorgonzola.

Seeing him coming, Gorgonzola emerged from his daze. He sprinted down the sidelines towards the goal. He crossed the goalline standing up. Wagner, still ten yards away, braked to a halt and shook his head in disgust.

For a long moment everything was very silent in Milhous Stadium. Everybody—fans, players, officials, coaches—was having trouble believing his eyes. Had the Whittier Stonewalls—zero points for thirty-six and three-quarters games—really scored a touchdown?

Pete Gorgonzola was the first to recover. He raised the ball high over his head and yelled "TOUCHDOWN!" He started to fling it to the ground and then caught himself. "TOUCHDOWN!" he yelled again. And he bent from the waist and laid it very gently in the mud of the end zone.

Pandemonium broke loose. The first one to reach Pete was a small brunette cheerleader named Taffy. I could hear her yelling all the way from the bench. "I'll move in with you, Pete," she was shouting. "We'll have a relationship. Maybe we'll even get married, have kids." Pete Gorgonzola looked pleased, but a bit overwhelmed. As for me, I felt pretty smug.

While the stadium security guards were clearing the astounded and exuberant fans from the field so that the game might proceed, I found myself watching Horseshoe Cohen, the field goal kicker I had counseled regarding his difficulty positioning his penis between his sex companion's labia. Horseshoe was carefully inserting the contact lenses I had recommended. Then, he positioned one of the cheerleaders about ten yards away from him and had her raise her short skirt. As usual, she wasn't wearing any panties. Holding the ball out in front of him, he lined up with her naked crotch and practiced placing his kicks. A little while later, Horseshoe scored the extra point, and Whittier was trailing only twenty-one to seven.

"Ain't that wonderful?" the cheerleader he'd been lining up with commented to me as she passed. "Put it in just as easy as last night."

Terry Bradshaw is possibly the most even-tempered player in professional football; nevertheless, his mouth was a grim, thin line when he trotted onto the field to take charge after the runback. It was even grimmer and thinner after the astounding second play.

On the first play, Steeler tight end Benny Cunningham had picked up five yards on an end run. As the teams lined up again, my eyes happened to light on Ambrose Pierce, the Whittier defensive lineman I had advised regarding penetrations of the neutral zone and premature ejaculation. He was muttering to himself. I read his lips.

"The only thing we have to fear is fear itself," he was repeating, under the impression that Ronald Reagan (who quoted it as fervently as if Franklin D. Roosevelt had been a right-wing Republican) had originated the phrase.

No matter. The ploy worked. Ambrose stayed on-side until the snap, following which his first move was precision-timed. He moved as if intending to charge over offensive guard Sam Davis. But the instant Davis committed himself to the straight-ahead confrontation, Ambrose slid smoothly around him to the left to shake up Bradshaw's timing in the slot.

The Steeler quarterback, looking for the short yardage that would give them the first down, had called a slant-out—a quick pass to tight end Randy Grossman out in the flat. The general ineptness of the Whittier defense, however, had lulled Bradshaw into expecting more time than Pierce's penetration now allowed. Bradshaw wasn't about to be sacked, but he did have to spin away from Pierce in order to fire the bullet.

Meanwhile, Sam Davis had recovered and came hurtling in to block Pierce from the side. Ambrose's concentration held, and he sidestepped the second block, although not quite so smoothly as he had the first. What happened then was one of those flukes that gridiron buffs talk about for years afterwards.

Ambrose saw a chance to dive over Davis and tackle Bradshaw. Sensing this, Davis rose straight up from the ground, erupting like a righteous volcano. He came up flush between Pierce's legs and Ambrose, flailing, locked his thighs around the guard's neck as he rose. Shaking himself, Davis broke the grip and Pierce went flying sidewise through space. He and Bradshaw's bullet pass to Grossman met in mid-air—converging vectors—and, when Ambrose Pierce hit the mud, the pigskin was lodged securely in his gut.

The turnover had the rain-soaked Whittier fans on their feet again. When they spotted Terry trotting out onto the field with the Whittier offense, they actually cheered. The team looked pleased but embarrassed. It was the first time their appearance had been greeted so enthusiastically.

Coach Newtrokni was a pixie play pusher. He sent Terry out with instructions to fire off the exact same sideline pass that had been intercepted from Bradshaw. It worked. The Whittier tight end, out in the flat, picked up exactly ten yards for the first down and stepped out of bounds to stop the clock. Terry Niemath, however, did not get off so easily in her success as Terry Bradshaw had in his failure. Remembering the long touchdown pass, the Steeler defense had paid their respects to the arm that had thrown it with an all-out blitz.

This time they nailed her. Twist as she would, Terry couldn't get away. A split second after the pass was fired, she went down under a saturation bombing of Pittsburgh blockbusters.

The pile-up included both linemen and backs. Middle linebacker Jack Lambert was the first to extricate himself from it. Immediately, the feared Steeler wild man began jumping up and down on the muddy field in an off-the-wall fashion which was decidedly uncool.

"A WOMAN!" It was a Tarzan yell to warn the natives of an alien presence in their jungle. "THE QUARTERBACK IS A @%!&ᶜ!⧸$!!! WOMAN!" (Later, there were some who claimed to have seen froth on Lambert's lips but, doubtless, they exaggerated.) "A WOMAN!!!"

The pile-up unraveled. Cornerback L. C. Greenwood walked away shaking his head disbelievingly. Jack Ham was looking at his hands and talking to himself as if he couldn't believe the answers they were giving him. Banaszak, who had been sprawled atop Terry and was the last up, slouched off with a face the color of an over-ripe tomato.

Lambert was still shouting and doing acrobatics in the mud. Steeler Coach Chuck Knoll, used to wild Jack's fierce shenanigans, at first ignored him. Finally, though, he marched onto the field to calm him down. A moment later it dawned on Knoll that Lambert wasn't horsing around and that the Whittier Stonewall quarterback was actually a female. Immediately Knoll started yelling for a referee so that he might lodge an official protest.

The two line judges reached the scene first. Considering the circumstances. Knoll was pretty calm in voicing his objections. He repeated them for the back judge and the downfield judges. When the umpire, whose authority was over-riding, joined them and Coach Knoll started in all over again, Coach Newtrokni decided it was time for him to join the fracas.

In the stands, still being pelted by raindrops, the fans had little appreciation of what the disturbance was all about. Used to Lambert's tumulting, they had given little credence to his shouts about a woman. Now they waited for the last quarter, which was half over, to resume.

"Is it true?" The umpire confronted Coach Newtrokni directly. "Is your quarterback Niemath of the female gender?"

"Yeah. So what?" Coach Newtrokni brazened it out.

"Women can't play professional football," the umpire told him.

"She's already playing."

"I mean, they're not allowed."

"Sez who?"

"Sez me!"

"How come?"

"It's against the rules!"

It was the statement Coach had been hoping would be made. "Oh, yeah?" He pulled a copy of the rulebook out of his hip pocket and handed it to the umpire. "Show me where in the rules it says any such thing."

The umpire leafed through the book. Chuck Knoll peered over his shoulder. Coach Newtrokni stood and tapped his foot. "Well?" he said finally.

"I can't find it," the umpire admitted.

" 'Cause it isn't there."

"Well, it would be if they'da thought it would ever come up."

"That's not good enough. There's nothing there stops my quarterback from playing. Let's get on with the game." He turned on his heel and headed back for the sidelines.

The umpire scratched his head. The line judges scratched their heads. The downfield judges scratched their heads. The back judge scratched his head. Finally, still scratching, they walked to their respective positions and signaled for the game to proceed.

For a moment it seemed as if Steeler Coach Chuck Knoll might refuse to let his team continue play against a woman. But then he shrugged his shoulders and went back to his side of the field. The shrug seemed to say that with the game almost over anyway and Pittsburgh ahead by fourteen points, there was no point in making an issue of it.

"Jeez! Look at Lambert." Beside me on the bench, defensive linebacker Freck Foley was worried. "He's got rabies! If the rest of their defense feel that way, they'll tear off Terry's tits."

"Not Mean Joe Greene." Grinder Meade spoke from Freck's other side. "He respects womanhood, little kids, and Coca Cola."

163

Aware of how rattled the Steeler defense must be, Coach sent in a play for Terry. Following it, she got off another long one to tight end Craig Cramp, who ran a post-hook pattern to the right. Loose as a goose since I'd guided him into water sports, Craig beat out cornerback Mel Blount and came up with the sphere for the Stonewalls' second TD. A couple of minutes later, Horseshoe Cohen kicked the extra point to make the score Steelers twenty-one, Whittier fourteen.

It was fantastic for the Stonewalls, of course, but time was running out in the last quarter, and it was Pittsburgh that was lining up to receive. Running back Sidney Thornton gathered in the pigskin on the Steeler seventeen, lowered his head like an angry bull, and started upfield through the mud as if his orders came straight from General Patton and the Whittier goal-line were the River Rhine. Skill, luck, mud, and a driving downpour were all on his side. A fake here, a quick move there, three successive straightarms, and he was leaving Whittier defense players behind him in the mire like croquet wickets on a rained-out lawn. By the time he crossed the fifty, more than half the Whittier defense was sprawled out on their face in his wake.

Blockers took out Freck Foley and Simon Sabbath, and Thornton crossed the forty and then the thirty. The only thing between him and a touchdown now was Whittier tackle Grinder Meade. Coming in from the side, Grinder committed himself at the twenty. Thornton twisted away and his lethal arm shot out. Grinder instinctively ducked the straight-arm, managing to bump Thorton, but not getting a grip on him. The jolt, however, was enough to make the mud-slick ball pop out of Thornton's clutch. It shot up behind him, Grinder got under it, and grabbed it just long enough to insure possession before Thornton reversed their positions and brought him down with a tackle. Through the rain I saw one of the referees signal that it was Whittier's ball on their own seventeen.

"What a break! What a break!" The s.a.c. was pounding the f.a.c. on the back.

The f.a.c. dampened his enthusiasm somewhat by pointing to the clock. The two-minute warning had gone by while the play was in progress. There was now a minute fifty-one left in the game.

Two plays later, there was a minute four left and Terry had not managed to budge them from their seventeen. Both long passes she had thrown had been batted down. The Steeler defense wasn't taking any chances. They were playing her deep and concentrating on the possible receivers.

So now, it was third and ten on the Whittier seventeen, and the clock was ticking. No matter that the defense was onto her. Terry had no choice but to call an option play which gave her two down-field receivers to choose between.

Her blocking held, and she had plenty of time to throw, but it was obvious that the defense was all over the wide receivers. She could throw the ball away, in which case the next play would be fourth and ten and they'd have to kick, or she could run with it. Terry chose to run.

She twisted away from the three-man rush,

doubled back to avoid Mean Joe Greene coming up the other side, and found a hole that left her in the open for a sure first down. It would have been no more than that had not Jack Lambert become the latest player to fall victim to the mud. His tackle turned from a *fait accompli* to a pratfall, and Terry was once again in the clear. Her next serious challenge came at the Steeler twenty from Mel Blount and, when he hesitated for a fraction of a second (later, Mel told reporters it was because he'd never before tackled a woman during a game), she twisted away from him. She was too fast for Mike Wagner to reach her before she crossed the goal line for the Stonewalls' third TD.

With thirty-two seconds left to play, Horseshoe Cohen fell into position with the team to kick the extra point. I noticed the cheerleader he'd been practicing with before drifting over to the fence behind the end zone. She positioned herself dead center between the goal posts, although well behind them. She raised her skirt. Raindrops glistened on her lush blue-black bush.

Horseshoe kicked. The ball landed right between her widespread legs. The kick was good. The score was twenty-one to twenty-one, and we were into sudden-death overtime.

"Wow, Coach! I'm speechless!" It was the only thing I could think of to say to congratulate him.

"Nothing to it." He winked. "We just got there Faustest with the mostest."

If our atheist coach had made a deal with the devil, however, old Beelzebub must not have been paying attention when the coin was tossed before the start of the overtime period. Bradshaw won the toss and, naturally, elected to receive. A disappointed sigh swept over the Whittier bench.

Despite the rain, the kick was a beauty. Thornton took it in his own end zone. The mud had slowed down the defense considerably, and so he had almost half a clear field in front of him. He elected to run with the ball.

There was no joy in Pittsburgh this day. And Sidney Thornton surely stood at the head of the joyless. On the one-yard line, his left foot encountered a mud-slick, and his butt hit the dirt. Even as he was recovering, the downfield judge was zooming in to call the ball dead.

Some situation! On the plus side for Pittsburgh, they had possession in sudden death overtime. On the minus side, their first-and-ten was on their own one-yard line. On the plus side, their quarterback was Terry Bradshaw, perhaps the coolest head in pro football, and he had the protection of an offensive line experienced in blocking as much weight as it could bench-press as well as three plays to make a first down, which would remove them from the goal-line situation.

Bradshaw took one step back with the snap—no more—positioning himself just behind his own goal line. Within the next two seconds, several other things happened at the same time. Ambrose Pierce valiantly faced off with Pittsburgh center Mike Webster. Number Thirty-two, Franco Harris, crossed behind Bradshaw to take the handoff. The handoff was blocked from the view of Hans Brinker (the Whittier middle linebacker I thought I'd cured of plugging the wrong hole by recommending anal sex) by his own lineman. Thinking Bradshaw still had possession, Brinker rushed to stop up an obvious opening through which Number Twelve might have slipped.

The blitz was on and, in the split seconds all this was occuring, Brinker moved too hastily. The ever-treacherous mud snagged him, and his feet went out from under him. His pratfall was much worse than the one Thornton had taken earlier. It carried him on his back and across the mud like a greased pig on a sliding pond. In this position he slid right between the braced and widespread legs of the grunting, butting, contending Ambrose Pierce and Mike Webster and emerged behind the Steelers' goal line. He arrived just in time to trip up Franco Harris inadvertently as he started to run with the handoff.

Harris went down. The line judge's whistle blew. The play was dead. Whittier had scored a safety in sudden death overtime.

And that, kiddies, is how we beat the Pittsburgh Steelers twenty-three to twenty-one!

It was pandemonium, of course. The fans were sobbing on the field and mobbing the players. The offense formed a ring around Terry Niemath and managed to hustle her off to the locker room before the focus shifted from Hans Brinker to her.

Coach Newtrokni elbowed his way through the crowd towards the Pittsburgh bench and Steeler Coach Chuck Koll. I trailed along behind him, curious to see how he'd behave in victory. The two coaches met in the midst of the throng, embraced and shook hands.

"Great game," Knoll said sincerely. "You earned the win."

"Nonsense, Chuck," Coach Newtrokni replied. "You outplayed us all the way. There's only one reason we managed to pull it out."

"What's that?"

"Why, it was God's will, Chuck," Coach Newtrokni told him with a perfectly straight face. "The Lord was on our side."

It was pouring cats and dogs but, to my surprise, Coach Newtrokni was not struck by lightning.

CHAPTER NINE

The next day, we made front page headlines as far away as the *New York Times*, which ran the story right beside one headed "Reagan Denies Budget-cutting Fiscal Policy Responsible for Lepers' Business Failures." Two parallel columns covered the Stonewalls-Steelers upset and the debut of professional football's first woman quarterback. Inside the paper, an editorial discussed the implications for the sport, for women, and for the American way of life generally:

...As John F. Kennedy observed, "Life is not always fair." Certainly it has not been so in the *de facto* segregation which has kept women out of professional football. Now, however, there must be an agonizing reappraisal of this policy. Whatever the result of this reappraisal, there is no denying the shock of a feminist-inspired earthquake whose tremors are even now spreading beyond the gridiron and throughout the entire male sports world. Anxious hockey players are already vowing that they will not countenance any females' pucking around on the ice.

... And what does this event portend for the status of women generally? The National Organization of Women asserts that quarterback Terry Niemath's right to play football is inviolable. The Moral Majority views it as a dastardly attack on family values and feminine daintiness. This newspaper leans toward the opinion that women should be allowed to participate in pigskin activities, while reserving the right to staff our sports department according to our time-honored traditions of experience, seniority, and access to all-male locker rooms.

... There can be no doubt that this is one more indication of how the American way of life is changing. While change for the sake of change is surely not desirable, there is also nothing to be gained by stubborn resistance to change. In this spirit, one of reasonable compromise among reasonable men, this newspaper recommends giving women the right to participate in professional football, while feeling obliged to question the wiseness of allowing them on the playing field past the onset of the second trimester of pregnancy. Feminists will say that the right to decide rests with the individual woman, while anti-feminists may wish to bar women with child altogether. The reasonable man, however, will surely agree to the wisdom of a compromise designed to keep the pregnant out of the huddle once they begin to show.

During the following week, the controversy escalated, spilling over from the sports pages and the editorial pages. A suit was filed on behalf of a twelve-year-old girl in Connecticut challenging the local Little League rules barring her from participation on the football team. The Governor of a southern state vowed personally to stand in the locker room door and block it to keep any "gal" from invading the hallowed male premises of the State University gridiron program. An ad hoc organization of born again Sunbelt ladies issued a statement that "real women" would never engage in such roughhouse activities, only lesbians; an immediate response from women athletes spearheaded by Billie Jean King denied vehemently that participation in even the roughest sports was any indication of sexual preference; this in turn was attacked as "reactionary" by the Sappho League, which demanded that the contribution of lesbians to professional sport be recognized and that their entrance into professional football be expedited.

A spokesman for the Administration told the press that, while President Reagan didn't wish to become involved in the controversy, his views on the sanctity of motherhood, wifehood, and the family were well known, and it was therefore safe to assume that he would not want his son to marry a football player. Listener-sponsored Pacifica Radio reported this and tacked on an ironic reminder that Reagan's son was a ballet dancer. A group of male ballet dancers protested the inference that his occupation might somehow make him less interested in female quarterbacks. Gay Rights activists protested their lack of sensitivity to the contributions of gay dancers to the art of ballet. The brouhaha fizzled out when somebody remembered that the President's son was already married.

The *Washington Post* conducted a straw poll among public personalities on the topic of women in professional football and came up with the following responses:

Budget Director David Stockman: "There will be no government funding of abortions for football players, no matter how needy they claim to be."

William F. Buckley: "If women do not immediately withdraw from professional football, I shall form a group of minutemen to demand male membership in NOW, the D.A.R., and the Girl Scouts of America!"

Bella Abzug: "Congress should immediately push through a bill providing day care facilities for football-playing mothers."

Reverend Jerry Falwell: "God is not pleased."

Kate Millet: "Not true; She is delighted."

Muhammad Ali: "Let 'em play ball/The ladies so sweet/But they get in the ring/I knock 'em off their feet!"

Warren Beatty: "The truth is, I never made it with a quarterback."

Elizabeth Holtzman: "I support Terry Niemath's right to play football without reservation."

Phyllis Schafly: "It is an appalling example to women everywhere."

Mayor Ed Koch of the City of New York: "Which way did you say the wind was blowing?"

Jane Fonda: "We're negotiating for the rights to

Terry Niemath's life story. If we get them, I of course will play Terry, with Jim Plunkett standing in for me in the gridiron scenes. Terry Bradshaw will play himself, and Coach Newtrokni will be portrayed by Lily Tomlin."

Governor Hugh Carey of New York: "There will be no trade-in of Westway funds to purchase Terry Niemath for the New York Jets."

Jimmy Breslin: "Not much support for Society Carey's position in the ginmills of Queens."

Senator Edward Kennedy of Massachusetts: "As to the question of her right to play against them, the Patriots will simply have to cross that bridge when they come to it."

Governor Jerry Brown of California: "Don't bother me; I'm meditating."

Norman Mailer: "I'm thinking about doing a book on Terry Niemath just as soon as she kicks off."

Christie Hefner: "We're negotiating with the Stonewalls for our next center spread."

Professor William Shockley, controversial genetics planner: "We have not yet decided if Terry Niemath should be granted access to our superior sperm bank."

Rock superstar Mick Jagger: "A chick quarterback's cool, man. What's she on?"

Abbie Hoffman: "Terry Niemath is a CIA android."

Gore Vidal: "The whole issue is a tempest in a chamberpot."

Former Editor of *The Realist*, Paul Krassner: "He means a shitpot!"

There were also reactions from abroad:

Pope John Paul II: "Holy Mother Church takes no position on women in American professional football as long as they do not use birth control."

Ayatollah Khomeini: "In Iran we would cut off her breasts for playing without a face veil."

British Prime Minister Margaret Thatcher: "It simply is not done in England."

Israeli Prime Minister Menachem Begin: "Niemath? Is that a Jewish name?"

Soviet Premier Leonid Brezhnev: "The Russian government categorically denies that four female fullbacks have attempted to defect to the Houston Oilers."

The day after the Soviet Premier's statement, I came across an interview in the *Los Angeles Times* with the Secretary of the Baroquian Club. "While the Baroquians have no official connection with the Whittier Stonewalls," he told the interviewer, "it is true that some of our most prestigious members have both a financial and sentimental interest in the team and that these gentlemen have endorsed the signing of Ms. Terry Niemath as quarterback, a decision which obviously played a major role in last Sunday's victory over Pittsburgh."

In response to the interviewer's suggestion that there might be an inconsistency in the Baroquian Club's anti-female membership and hiring policies vis-a-vis the endorsing of a female quarterback, the Secretary had this to say: "No inconsistency at all. One thing has nothing to do with the other. We believe firmly that women have the right to participate in professional sports in accordance with their abilities. We also believe that we have the right of free association as a club and the right to limit that association as we see fit. Now, we see fit to limit it in such a way as not to inhibit our members in those theatrical activities which give them so much pleasure. Surely, you must see that nothing would be so inhibiting as to be gawked at by the very gender we have chosen to poke good-natured fun at. But—and this is important—we are not rigid. Not only have some of us used our considerable influence to inject a woman into professional football but, also, I personally am on a committee which is dickering with a young lady to pop naked out of a cake at our next Baroquian Club anniversary dinner, as a compromise of our tradition barring women employees on the premises. Now, I ask you, what could be more reasonable that that?"

Public debate continued right up until the following Sunday, when Terry Niemath played in her second game for Whittier, against the Denver Broncos. Over fifty-one thousand people filled Mile High Stadium to capacity. Whatever else one might say about a female pro football quarterback, the front office boys couldn't miss the fact that she was big box office.

Despite the victory over Pittsburgh, the Stonewalls went into the Denver game thirteen-point underdogs. The weather forecast was bright and sunny, and the smart money said that the Steelers had fallen victim to the mud, and that the Whittier victory over them had been a fluke.

Denver was a well-oiled machine which always worked best under solar power. The bright light of the sun was expected to decimate the Stonewalls and to melt away whatever dazzle their lady quarterback might have used to bewitch the Steelers.

Imagine the wise guys' chagrin when Terry turned out to be a Bronco-buster *par excellence*. She dug in her spurs, twisted their tails, and left them braying for mercy with four—count 'em, four!—touchdown passes that inspired the Whittier defense to dig in its heels and hold Denver down to a three-TD response. The final score was Whittier twenty-seven, Denver twenty-four, and just about every sports columnist around was wiping egg off his face.

"Congratulations," I told Terry sincerely when she returned to the Denver hotel room we were sharing after the game. "You looked great out there today."

"Y'all look again. I'm even greater right here in the privacy of our little ol' home away from home," she answered, shedding her clothes as she came across the rug towards me.

It had been like that all week. Since I'd moved in with Terry to protect the rest of the team from her advances, I'd been the focal point of her libido. It hadn't been easy holding her off. As Terry kept reminding me, it wasn't as if we hadn't made it together before. "Sex is a right friendly act," she kept reminding me. "Aren't we still friends?"

"Sure," I would answer. "But friendship is a delicate balance. We don't want to screw it up with sex."

177

The answer was incomprehensible to Terry. Truthfully, it was more than a little lacking in logic to me as well. As she upped her campaign with more aphrodisiac perfumes, flimsier nightgowns and more pronounced wrigglings, heavings and undulations, I was hard-pressed to justify to myself not making love to her.

The original problem had been that if she made it with various members of the team, it would cause dissension among them. Above all, Coach Newtrokni didn't want that. But I wasn't on the team. And, in point of fact, most of the guys took it for granted that I was making it with Terry, since we were rooming together. Nuke Outlaw, in particular, glowered at me whenever our paths crossed like Godzilla deprived of his mate.

Why, then, was I withholding my favors? I suppose, because I like to think of myself as a professional in my chosen field. A professional does not become involved on a personal level. Such involvement invariably undermines effectiveness. If I was going to ride herd on Terry, then I had to maintain some distance between us no matter what had transpired previously; thus, frustration was a matter of honor, and blue balls the badge of my status.

All of which didn't make it any easier now, after the Bronco game, when Terry, fresh from the showers, all powdered and perfumed, wriggled out of her panties and winked her pussy at me. "What say we celebrate, Steve, ol' buddy," she suggested, stroking my thigh.

"I have to take a shower." I backed off towards the bathroom. "A *cold* shower."

I stayed in the shower until I was sure she'd gone out for dinner. Then I went out myself. I made sure it was very late when I came back so that Terry would be asleep. I contrived to crawl into the empty twin bed without waking her. Ignoring my erection, I managed to drift off to sleep myself.

Some time later, I was awakened by the sounds of sobbing coming from Terry's bed. I switched on the night light on the side away from her. In the dimness of its gentle glow, I could see that she was quite sound asleep and obviously having a disturbing dream."

"Yes!" she moaned. "No!" She opened her mouth wide and formed an 'O' with her lips. "Mmm!" she sighed. "And then: "I surely do not want any onions, lover!" She began crying, as if with frustration.

It was heartrending. I stood it as long as I could, thinking the dream might change. But in the end I reached across to Terry's bed and shook her gently by her smooth and rounded naked shoulder.

"AAGGHH!" She screamed and sat bolt upright in bed. It took a moment for her eyes to focus. When they did, she looked at me and burst into tears.

"Terry! What is it?" I crossed over to her bed and sat on the edge. "What's the matter?"

The sound of my voice, however, only seemed to inspire her to a greater flow of tears. I couldn't stand it. Women's tears are a universal solvent to the will. My resistance to Terry dissolved on the spot. For the past week I had avoided physical contact with her, but now I took her in my arms to

179

comfort her.

"What is it?" I repeated.

"I had me a dream." Finally she managed to get it out between sobs.

"Tell me about it."

"It was about you-all." She snuggled closer, her breasts warm and springy against me through the thin nightgown. "Sort of," she amended.

"Sort of?" I prompted her.

"It was up north at that Shea Stadium, but I wasn't rightly playin'." She took a handkerchief from me and blew her nose. "Y'all might say I was more like a spectator."

"I see." I smoothed her short blonde hair from her brow. "What happened in the dream, Terry?"

"I was a-watchin' the football game when a vendor came along with this here tray of hot dogs. Big, long weenies like they have sometimes, you know?"

"I've seen them."

"Lordy, I wanted me one of them! I mean my mouth was purely waterin'! In the dream, that is. Fact is, in real life, I ain't much for that Yankee food."

"Stick to the dream."

"Alrighty. Well, in the dream, eager as I was, I paid the vendor and I reached out to take me one of them frankfurters. Only—Only—"

"Only?"

"Only when I picked up the roll, it didn't come free like you'd rightly 'spect it would."

"I don't get it. What do you mean?"

"It was attached."

"Attached how?"

"The weenie was attached to the vendor. It was lying' there all long an' red an' juicy in the roll, but it wasn't a hot dog at all. No, sir! That there frankfurter was really his pecker."

"Freud be praised!"

"What was that y'all said, Steve?"

"Never mind. Go on with the dream."

"Well, now, realizin' this, I all of a sudden was hungrier even than afore. I wanted that thang so bad! So bad I could rightly taste it! An' that's what I said to that there vendor. 'Gimme my frank!' I said. 'Give it here!' "

"Then what happened?"

"The vendor, he asked did I want mustard on it. I said real polite. 'Yes, thank you kindly.' Then he asks do I want sauerkraut an' I tell him no. He goes to hand me the pecker-in-a-roll, an' my mouth gets real big an' round like I'm gonna suck this weenie steada eatin' it. Anyway, he pulls it back, like he's teasin' me, an' he says do I want onions on it. One thang I hate on a hot dog, it's onions! That is pure-ly a Yankee trick!" Suddenly she was crying again.

"It was only a dream." I tried to console her.

"I began a-suckin' on that weenie an' it was so good! So good!" She was half incoherent. "My box was on fire an' I was rubbin' it 'tween my legs there in the bleachers an' a-suckin' away when—when—"

"Take it easy."

"Suddenly, this here vendor, he pulls it out of my mouth an' begins a-laughin' at me like the devil hisself. But that wasn't all. That wasn't the worst. The worst—The worst—"

"Shh, baby. It was only a dream."

"No, it wasn't! It was the way it is! Just the way it is!"

"What do you mean?"

"That there devil-vendor's face—His face when he took that pecker I wanted so bad plumb out of my lovin' mouth—His face—"

"Easy, baby."

"His face was your face, Steve! Your face! You were him! An', just like always, you were pullin' your pecker away from me!" Once again, her wailing dissolved into incoherence.

Can you dig it, guys? Sigmund? August? Ingmar? All aboard! First stop dreamland, next stop guilt. My guilt! Well, hell, hadn't my holding out on her driven Terry to dreaming such a textbook dream? And wasn't it my responsibility to kiss it and make it better?

Yeah, that's what I did. So much for professionalism, and the devil take the hindmost. I kissed the tears from her wet cheeks. I kissed the frustration from her lips. I kissed away the hunger and the emptiness. I kissed and made it better.

Terry's arms went around my neck and she clung to me. Her wet cheeks glistened. The silk of her nightgown rose and fell quickly. Her blue eyes were grateful and filled with desire. Her mouth moved over mine with lips that were warm and moist and a tongue that was electric and probing. "So good!" she sighed. "This here is so rightly good!"

The throbbing of my cock confirmed her judgment. I had been sleeping in only my jockey shorts, and now it stuck out between us unshamedly—aroused, stiff, and arrogant. Looking own from lowered lids through spiderweb lashes, erry saw it and caught her breath. Her hand ropped from my neck and encircled its nakedness. "My weenie!" Her laugh was low and throaty. My hot dog!"

"Without sauerkraut."

"Without mustard."

"Without onions."

"Praise be to the Lord! I surely do hate onions! ou Yankees are plumb crazy puttin' such a thing n your weenies." She slid down my body and ulled down my shorts. "Delicious!" She fondled y cock and kissed it. Then she started playing ith my balls.

I noticed that she wasn't crying any more, but hat didn't make me back off. I was past that point. Ier lips and tongue, teasing my hard-on, left me elpless to reverse the action.

My hands moved as if there had never been any uestion. They slid down her milky shoulders and osom and under her breasts. These were heavy nd hot as I squeezed and stroked them. The sunanned flesh glowed pale gold in the lamplight, and 'erry's large, strawberry-shaped nipples stood out tiff and hungry-red. When I palmed them, she loaned and took one of my balls between her lips, easing its hairiness with her tongue, sucking it as if t was some particularly delectable piece of hard andy.

"I surely do have the most sensitive titties," she onfessed, lifting her pursed mouth for a moment. "Nothin' I wouldn't do for a man if 'n he plays with 'em just right." She extended her tongue well under my balls and tickled my asshole with it.

Reaching down, I pulled her around so that her long, sturdy, shapely legs extended beyond my head and over the edge of the bed. The sensually sculpted cheeks of her delicious behind quivered and shimmered. Gently, unable to resist, I sank my teeth into the rose-gold flesh.

"Oooh!" She drew the length of my cock deep down her throat and sucked hard at the base with velvety, cunning lips. "Mmm!"

I spread her thighs apart, my fingertips tracing the flexed muscles of their insides and savoring the excited beating of the pulse there. The curly blonde hair of her quim was dewy and fragrant. Swollen purple lips opened to my mouth. The sweetest of female creams widened the walls of her inner pussy for my tongue. I found her clit and licked it slowly—teasing her, arousing her even more.

Her strong hot thighs tightened around my ears. In the mirror across from the bed I saw my cock rising like a flagpole, disappearing in Terry's wide-stretched, lascivious mouth, and then reappearing hard and throbbing and glistening with her saliva. She was crouched over me, and her large breasts were hanging down, the excited tips sweeping back and forth over my belly and groin as she moved. Now, as I watched in the mirror, she took one in her hand and worked the nipple around my balls. She took my cock out of her mouth and pressed her nipple against its crest. She forced the hard red berry into the lust-widened hole of my prick. When she removed it there was a sheen of premature jizzum over it.

I plunged my tongue all the way up her cunt. I sucked the juices from her writhing pussy. I pumped my cock in and out of her mouth.

"Wait!" Terry pulled away panting. "I want y'all to fuck me. Please! Please! Please! Y'all do me proper!" She scrambled around on the bed and straddled me, holding herself high so that her now slavering pussy was suspended over the tip of my thrusting, swollen prick.

I reached up and found one of her large, firm breasts. I sucked as much of it into my mouth as I could. I licked and nibbled at the juicy strawberry nipple.

Terry's sharp nails clawed at the back of my neck. Her ass jutted high and backwards once and then slammed forwards. Her meaty quim slammed down on my pecker and spread out over my pelvis. She moved up and down, contriving to have the erect button of her clitty ride the length of my shaft.

I reached around her with both hands and clutched the burning, trembling cheeks of her behind. I widened the cleft there and dipped with my middle finger. The sensation drove Terry berserk. Her tight cunt wrenched at my cock and she jerked left and right wildly and slammed her cunt down harder and harder in order to feel the full length of my perpendicular prick all the way up her lusting tunnel.

"Y'all are a sly bastard!" she panted. "Tricky! A-suckin' my titties like this an' sneakin' up my no-no all at the same time you doin' me! Yessir! Sly an' tricky!'' She reached behind her, stretched her arm down the length of her back and contrived to palm my pumping balls.

I watched her fondle and squeeze them in the mirror as the length of my cock moved in and out of her bouncing quim. She strained her head to look over her shoulder to see what I was looking at. When she saw the reflection of us fucking, Terry emitted a sound that was half-laugh and half-groan. Continuing to stare, she redoubled her efforts, moving up and down faster and faster, fucking harder and harder and hotter and hotter.

"Come on!'' she gasped. "Give it to me! Y'all lemme have that geyser of hot cream all the way up my hungry pussy!''

I shoved my finger up her ass and pulled her down hard on me. I sank my teeth into the damp flesh of her breast and sucked the strawberry nipple down my throat. I clawed at her ass and felt the pressure of the jizzum rising from my balls to fill the length of my cock. I held back, agonizingly, until I felt the muscles inside her pussy forming clutch-ridges around my shaft. There was a melting deep inside Terry and then she was screaming incoherently with the release—a gushing sensation—of her orgasm. I let go then, pumping hard and brutal, shooting high up her quim, releasing one hot spurt after another until her sucking cunt overflowed and we ended our orgasm soaked with the juices of our lust.

That first time was not, of course, the last time. Once I'd succumbed to the temptation, there was no holding back from further indulgence. Besides, Terry claimed that regular balling helped her game.

"I'll bet." I had been skeptical at first.

"It truly does, Steve darlin'."

"How? Give me a for-instance."

"Friggin' you, for instance. Now that's helped me develop a real smooth rhythm for hand-offs."

"I'll just bet!"

"An' my broken field runnin' is surely improved."

"What's that have to do with our balling?"

"Why, the way I move my hips, darlin'. Haven't you noticed? Every time I see a tackle comin', I just pretend you're jumpin' on my bones from behind an' give my bottom that special wiggle an' shake him off."

"Don't forget fakes." I teased her.

"Not true. Y'all know I never fake in bed. But you have helped my passin', sugah. Truly you have."

"In what way?"

"I'm more relaxed in the pocket."

"I noticed." I was being sarcastic.

"I truly am. And our lovemakin' has taught me patience, so I don't fire off my passes too soon."

"You never know what that old O.R.G.Y. expertise is going to accomplish."

"Fact is, our sack time's improved my timing all around."

The funny thing is that what she said had more than a little truth to it. As time passed, Terry's performance on the gridiron was looking more and more professional. Also, like a pebble in a brook, it was throwing off ripples of inspiration which were positively affecting the other members of the Whittier Stonewalls.

The offense began operating as a cohesive unit. The blockers gained the confidence to take on the largest defensive lines in the league. The wide receivers developed an almost religious faith in Terry's ability to get the ball to where it was supposed to be and, along with it, they began to have faith in themselves to be there to catch it. Even our ground game improved as the offensive backs realized that there really were holes there for them to plunge through. Morale mounted, and there were fewer fumbles and more smoothly unified plays.

The team spirit spread to the defense, as well. With wins under their belt, they seemed to develop a sense of obligation not to relinquish the gains provided by Terry and the other offensive players. They began reading the opposition plays more accurately and quickly. They took more risks, moved more quickly to break up pass plays, and hit harder. And they began piling up a quite acceptable record of both sacks and interceptions.

All this was adding up to one victory after another for Terry Niemath and the Whittier Stonewalls. The Colts, the Browns, and the Chargers all went down to defeat. Nor was there any joy in Buffalo, Cincinnati, or Kansas City after the Stonewalls came to town. The season moved right along, and still we were undefeated.

The teams we faced were not the only ones who had to make an effort to adapt to a woman quarterback with all-around playing ability. Their cheerleading squads also had to evolve a strategy aimed at dissipating Terry's Superwoman image. "Hold that blonde!" and "Hit her again, harder! Harder!" were not enough. Soon the various cheerleading squads had developed special cheers specifically aimed at exorcising Terry's gridiron magic. For instance:

"HIT HER IN THE LEFT TIT! HIT HER IN THE RIGHT! HIT HER IN THE BOX AND FIGHT, TEAM, FIGHT!

And,

"SUNNY OR SHADY, WATCH HER ASS! SPREAD THAT LADY ON THE GRASS!"

Also, in a Nietzschean vein—

"HIP! HIP! HIP! LET 'ER RIP! WOMAN PASSING? USE THY WHIP!"

Nor were the cheerleaders the only ones forced to adjust to Terry's presence on the gridiron. At the highest levels of professional football, the grand pundits of the game were engaging in a bitter debate regarding the rule changes necessary to accommodate female players. Their arguments spilled over into the press and, soon, the fans were taking sides.

Hard-liners thought that new rules should be instituted to limit the effect of women on those against whom they played. More pliable fans, less threatened by the toppling of tradition, thought the rule changes should concentrate on providing women some special protections in keeping with their femininity. The debaters voiced their views as follows:

"Their breasts should be bound to flatten them,

so they don't distract the guys on the other team."

"A ten-yard penalty should be instituted for holding a woman player above the waist."

"Wiggling should be declared illegal motion!"

"Fifteen yards for groping a female in the pile-up."

"If a chick quarterback gets caught flashing, she should be thrown out of the game."

"They should automatically penalize 'em half the distance to the goal line for buggering a female tight end."

Sports announcers were also having problems dealing with a woman player. Commenting on Terry's games, more than once they found themselves trapped into *double entendres*. For instance:

"Fumble! And, making the recovery, Terry Niemath goes down on it like a real pro!"

"When it comes to fly patterns, this lady quarterback sucks 'em in every time!"

"They have to play deep and hard, and so she always has that defense breathing heavy!"

"Few quarterbacks can lay 'em down like Terry Niemath does!"

"Ahead or behind, Terry just keeps banging away!"

Aside from game coverage, TV took cognizance of Terry in other ways. Suddenly there were women appearing in the formerly all-male commercials slotted into the time-outs. Lissome blonde kickers shaved their long legs for Gillette. Curvy, bosomy brunette linebackers arm-wrestled for light beers. A redheaded defensive guard with hips like Raquel

Welch's did a Dannon Yogurt ad with a male ballet dancer famous for his *entrechats*. An Afro-American beauty in the bedraggled post-game uniform of a defensive left tackle accepted a coke from a starry-eyed waif-fan and tossed the kid her sweaty bra by way of appreciation. Inevitably, Terry herself was signed up to do a commercial.

It was for a manufacturer of sanitary napkins. "I never have to worry no matter how rough the game gets," Terry informed the viewing audience. "I'm always secure in the knowledge that I have the utmost in feminine protection." The video accompanying her voice-over showed Terry taking three tackles, one right after the other, all in the crotch. Then, there was a quick fade-out and fade-in to show her in organdy drinking champagne with a guy in a tuxedo against a background that was all candlelight and soft focus. "I may be a football player," Terry confided, "but I'm a woman, too." The guy kissed her hand, and she sighed. "Just like you," she told all those women stuck with husbands nailed down in front of the Sunday afternoon football game.

The day that particular commercial debuted, Terry's arm propelled the Whittier Stonewalls into contention for the Western Division championship. The playoff game was set for the following Sunday. It was a stunning achievement for the Stonewalls. We'd started the season in the cellar and here we were with a shot at being Number One. If we made it, that meant the Superbowl. Most of us didn't even dare think about that out loud.

Charles Putnam called me. He wanted to tell me

that he and his associates were delighted with my handling of the Terry Niemath situation. If we took the Division championship, there would be a bonus in it for me. And, if we won the Superbowl—well, perhaps it was premature to look that far ahead, but he could assure me that I would be a very happy man. Even if we should fall short of that, he wanted me to know that the gentleman from Whittier was out of his depression and proud as a peacock of the team established in his honor. "He hasn't been in such high spirits since the bombing of Cambodia," Putnam assured me.

His call was followed by the news that Terry Niemath had been named "Woman of the Year" by SWAP (Sensual Women Against Pornography). Stephanie Greenwillow, one of the founding members and an officer of the organization, was coming to Whittier to present Terry with a scroll honoring her. Despite our falling out, I couldn't help looking forward to seeing Stephanie again.

An unexpected happenstance, however, spoiled my anticipation. It occurred the night of the win that put Whittier in the playoffs. I had made a date with Rhino Dubrowski to go out and have a few drinks to celebrate. Rhino, however, had gotten a head start on me, and so, along about nine in the evening, I found myself putting him to bed, and our celebration was aborted. I've never been one for celebrating by myself, and so I decided, the hell with it, and went to my room to hit the sack early.

Terry, obviously, wasn't expecting me. I walked in on her and Grinder Meade performing the old in-out with the kind of energy you might expect from runaway slaves hotfooting it across the ice-floes with the bloodhounds at their heels. Grinder's ebony ass was going like he could feel their fangs snapping.

"What the hell do you call this?" I exclaimed.

"Y'all mean you can't tell?" Terry panted, not even bothering to stop.

It was pointless trying to lay a guilt trip on her. "Grinder!" I tried him. "You know this is against the rules!"

"You got to be kidding, boy!" Grinder wasn't buying it.

"You think this is right?"

"Miz Scarlett here ain't hardly complainin'." Grinder was both sarcastic and undeterred.

I closed the door on them and went back downstairs to the bar. Sometimes, drinking alone isn't so bad after all. My only complaint was the hangover I had the next day when I bumped into Grinder in the hallway. "I'm surprised at you," I told him, my liquor-dulled brain incapable of much more by way of an opening line.

"It bother you 'cause I'm black?" He towered over me, but his voice was more sad than hostile.

"No. It bothers me because it's not good for the team."

"You mean good for the team like when you fuck the lady?"

"That's different," I rationalized. "I'm not on the team."

"Oh! I see! You're all upset 'cause somebody on the team is balling her."

"That's right." I had too much of a hangover to

keep the self-righteousness out of my voice.

"Well, then, you'd best get un-upset. 'Cause, you see, Steve boy, everybody on the team, black and white together, has been ballin' the quarterback in the locker room all season."

"Why didn't anybody tell me about this?" I demanded.

"We figured you were getting yours in a nice soft bed, so why bother you with the seamier side of locker room life?"

"Listen, Grinder, if you're telling the truth, we're all in trouble! Can you imagine what Coach Newtrokni's going to do when he finds out?"

"He ain't goin' to do nothing!"

"How do you figure that?"

"Hell, Victor, he's the one said we shouldn't bother telling you we were all fucking her."

"You mean the coach is screwing her too?"

"Hell, it was him set up the schedule for the team, and you'd best believe he wasn't getting no sloppy seconds."

So much for duty! So much for professionalism! So much for the Organization for the Rational Guidance of Youth!

For the rest of that week, I brooded over how I'd been had. I'd thought I was servicing Terry in order to maintain the team's equilibrium. I'd thought I was at least partially responsible for the team morale that had brought us victory after victory. And all the time it had been Terry screwing the whole team, as always, which had been behind it. I brooded . . . oh, how I brooded!

The presentation of the SWAP award was Saturday evening, the night before the playoff game. Terry dressed in virginal white to receive it. Stephanie was wearing a particularly sexy green evening gown.

Watching them up there together on the dais, I was struck by how much alike they were physically. Despite the fact that Terry weighed about ten pounds more, their heights and builds were identical to the eye. The ten pounds was all hidden muscle. They were both bosomy, long-legged, and pinch-waisted. They both had hips made for lovemaking and high, beautifully sculpted *derrieres*. Terry had short blonde hair and blue eyes, while Stephanie's tresses were long and red and her eyes jade green but, nevertheless, their faces resembled each other. They had the same high cheekbones, full, erotic lips, and firm tilted jawlines. They could easily have been sisters.

Sisterhood, however, has its limits. This is true even for the most dedicated feminists. I learned that after the ceremony, when Stephanie and I found ourselves alone together while Coach Newtrokni and Terry, with whom we were sharing a table, were dancing.

"Are you sleeping with her?" Stephanie asked me, her green eyes flashing true to their nature.

"Of course not!" I lied with real indignation in my voice.

She stared at me and said nothing.

"Why are you looking at me that way?"

"Your nose just grew three full inches, Pinnochio."

"I don't see that it's any of your business

anyway. You said you were through with me."

"I am." Stephanie sighed. "I miss you, you bastard!"

"Yeah. Well, I miss you, too."

And so, of course, we went to bed together.

I almost blew it while we were undressing. "Why," I wondered, "did your group give Terry Niemath, of all people, an award for her contribution to the fight for women's rights?"

"Because she's the first woman in organized football."

"But she's not interested in women's rights. She's only interested in screwing."

"That's a woman's right, too," Stephanie murmured.

I bit my tongue and let it go at that. She was naked. It was a time to make love, so that's what we did. It was great.

The next day, Terry completed nineteen for twenty-seven. The Whittier Stonewalls won the playoff game twenty-eight to fourteen. Next stop, the Superbowl!

That night, Terry Niemath disappeared!

CHAPTER TEN

"What the hell do you mean, she disappeared?" Coach Newtrokni demanded.

"She never came back to her room last night," I told him.

"Maybe she met some guy and she's shacking up with him."

"Could be." I shrugged. "Only she's never done that before. Probably," I added maliciously, "because she was getting enough around here."

"Maybe she wanted variety." Coach was optimistic.

"Yeah, Victor." Nuke Outlaw threw me the zinger. "Rooming with you, that's probably what she wanted all right."

"She's never missed the post-game movies before," Rhino pointed out while the tackle and I exchanged glares. "And it's already cohabitating afternoon and she hasn't called or anything."

"Let's get on with the flicks," Coach decided. "Maybe she'll turn up."

But she didn't turn up. Not that afternoon. Not that night. And not the next day, either.

"Where's your star quarterback?" the sports reporter wanted to know at Tuesday practice.

"Coach was so happy with her performance Sunday that he gave her the day off," the Stonewalls' publicity man told him.

Obviously, we could only get away with that excuse once. With the Superbowl game less than two weeks off, more and more attention would be focused on Whittier every day. If it came out that our star quarterback was missing, there was bound to be a furor in the press.

Late Tuesday night, Rhino and I went to Coach Newtrokni's room to discuss the situation. We were a little puzzled to find the team physician waiting there with Coach. What did he have to do with Terry's disappearance?

"Tell them what you told me, Dr. Fink," Coach instructed him.

"I examined Terry Niemath the day before the playoff game," he told us. "I have a friend at the local lab, so I got the results of certain tests back very quickly. I told Terry what they were just after the game on Sunday."

"That was just before she disappeared," Coach Newtrokni pointed out.

"What kind of tests and what kind of results?" I asked with a sinking stomach.

"Pregnancy tests," Dr. Fink replied.

"And?"

"Terry Niemath was pregnant."

"Why don't you call the rest of the team in here?" I suggested to Coach Newtrokni. "We could all congratulate each other on our impending fatherhood."

"Pregnant!" Rhino exclaimed. "Feces! That must be why she took off."

"It's gonna be one helluva paternity suit!" I realized.

"It's the logical explanation." Coach Newtrokni responded to Rhino and ignored me. "The question is, now that she's gone, what do we do?"

"Maybe she went to get an abortion." Rhino looked on what he thought was the bright side. "Maybe she'll come back after and play in the Superbowl."

"Will she be able to?" Coach asked Dr. Fink.

"Perhaps. With the right drugs . . . We've done worse things medically in pro football . . . Of course, I'd have to examine her first . . ."

"Then you have to. find her," Coach decided, looking straight at Rhino and me. "And meanwhile, we have to think of something to keep the press off our backs about her not being at practice."

"Like what?" I was dubious.

There was a long silence. Rhino broke it with a snap of his fingers. "A ringer!" he suggested. "What we need is a maternal-mating ringer!"

"Where are we going to get a quarterback like Terry to be a ringer?" I wanted to know.

"Season's over. I'll bet any one of the pro quarterbacks would do it for the right price."

"I can't think of one who's built like Terry," I reminded him.

"In drag," Rhino offered optimistically.

"Rhino, you've got to get over the idea that people who watch football—even practice sessions—are blind. You can't pass a woman off as a man on the football field, and it won't work vice versa either."

"Right idea. Wrong approach." Coach shut us both up.

"What do you mean?" we asked him, speaking in tandem.

"What we need is a woman ringer to stand in for Terry. Someone who looks like her enough so that, if we put a uniform on her and a helmet and don't let anybody too close, it'll fool the press."

"It'll only fool them until she gets on the field," I pointed out. "As soon as this woman throws a pass, they'll know it isn't Terry."

"This ringer won't have to throw a pass. She won't have to do anything. She won't even have to go on the field. All she'll have to do is sit on the bench."

"How come?"

"Because we're going to leak it that Terry has a back injury that temporarily keeps her from passing or running. We'll say that it'll be okay by Superbowl Sunday, but that meanwhile, Terry has to take it easy."

"That'll wreak Hades with the point spread," Rhino commented.

"So what?" Coach Newtrokni shrugged. "It can't hurt us to go into the Superbowl the under-

200

dog. It won't be the first time this year the experts have figured us to lose. The big question is, where do we find a woman who looks enough like Terry to pass for a ringer and who'll be willing to do it?"

"I think I have the answer to that," I heard myself saying.

"Who?" Rhino, Coach, and Dr. Fink all wanted to know.

Who? Why, Stephanie Greenwillow, of course. Who else?

She wasn't exactly easy to persuade. "Why should I?" was her immediate reaction.

"Sisterhood," I suggested. "Here's a sister in trouble. Pregnant. In need of help. This is how you can help her."

"I don't even know her."

"I've heard it said that the women's movement was too theoretical and had no real empathy for poor women beset by the realities of the real world. Of course, I never believed it, but ..."

"That's nonsense! Terry Niemath isn't a poor woman. On the contrary, her income is way above that of most working women."

"She's a symbol, an important symbol to women everywhere. Her breakthrough into pro football is a major step forward for women. Do you want her accomplishment obscured by the irrelevant facts of pregnancy and possible abortion if it comes out why she's not at practice?"

"You really think I could pass for her?" Stephanie weakened.

"If we cut your hair short and dye it blonde, it

201

shouldn't be any problem."

"What about the other members of the team?"

"Don't worry about them. They'll keep their mouths shut."

"You mean because of their possible paternity?"

"Nope. I mean because they're hungry for their shares of the Superbowl pot. Their only chance at the winning pie is if Terry plays. If it comes out that Terry's been pregnant and had an abortion, there very likely would be an outcry that could keep her from playing. That would hit the rest of the team right smack in the pocketbook."

"I'm not so sure it would be right for her to play myself."

"Isn't that her decision? I mean you're always talking about how women should have control over their own bodies. Isn't the overriding feminist policy that Terry should have the right to decide for herself whether or not to play?"

"I suppose so," Stephanie granted reluctantly.

"Then you'll do it? You'll cover for her?"

"I have all kinds of reservations." Stephanie took a deep breath. "But I'll do it."

In uniform and helmet, it was really impossible to tell Stephanie from Terry at a distance. The entire team cooperated in seeing that the sports press was kept at just that from Stephanie—a distance. In other ways, however, they weren't so cooperative. Rhino, Coach Newtrokni, and I perceived this when we walked into the locker room after practice and faced a scene of violence and chaos.

Stephanie was backed against a locker with her

202

jersey off and her proud breasts heaving and beckoning in naked splendor. She had half of a broken stool clutched in both hands and was waving it threateningly over her head. The three aisles converging on where she was standing were strewn with injured players.

"What the hell's going on?" Coach Newtrokni demanded.

"They tried to rape me!"

"Who tried to rape you? Be specific."

"I am being specific. They did. All of them."

"What the hell's the matter with you guys?" Coach was indignant.

"We didn't try to rape her, Coach." Linebacker Freck Foley was the first to speak up in the team's defense.

"No, sir!" kicker Horseshoe Cohen chimed in. "All we did was party like always. You know, like with Terry."

"They all took out their organs and went for me." Stephanie was furious.

"Terry never minded," Plowboy Palmer remembered.

"They were all stiff!"

"That was a compliment, Ma'am," Grinder Meade told her. "Wasn't no call for you to take on so."

"Just look what she done to me, Coach!" Wide receiver Pete Gorgonzola held up his genitals. They were bruised and swollen. "Whacked 'em with that chair leg she's swinging. Hell, you call that ladylike?"

"I am not a lady!" Stephanie snarled. "I'm a

woman who's not about to let herself be gang-banged!"

"How many injuries are there?" Coach was concerned.

"Eight down, sir." The f.a.c. had computed rapidly.

"Jesus!" Coach Newtrokni was shocked. "What are you trying to do to me, lady? Don't you know these men have to play in the Superbowl a week from Sunday? And why in the groin? Don't you know groin injuries shake up their confidence worse than any other kind of injury?"

"They deserved it for attacking me!"

"We wasn't attacking her! We was just being friendly like we always was with Terry!"

"I'm not Terry! I'm not friendly! I'm not available for sex!"

"Oh, yeah?" Nuke Outlaw was skeptical. "How about him?" His gargantuan finger was pointing at me.

"What about him?"

"You room with him just like Terry did. You trying to tell us you're not balling him?"

"Not anymore, I'm not!" Stephanie assured him. "What's past is past and, while I'm with this team, I'm not going to have sex with anyone! And that includes Steve!"

"I know you had to say that, Stephanie," I told her when we were alone in our room later that night. "But, of course, you didn't mean it. Right?"

"Wrong! I meant every word of it."

"Now, Stephanie, let's not be rigid . . ."

"Let's not *you* be rigid!" She waved a lamp in the general direction of the erection sticking out of my shorts. "I'm serious, Steve! One more step, and I'll do to you what I did to those eight guys on the team this afternoon!"

I made the mistake of taking that one step more. The lamp zinged for my exposed and rigid penis like a missile homing in on its target. I had no choice but to take evasive action. This consisted of hightailing it from the room and closing the door between me and Stephanie's deadly aim. I held onto the knob so she couldn't open it for another shot at my wanton wang.

"Mr. Victor!" the voice came from the hallway behind me. "I have to see you."

I wheeled around and found myself facing Bubba Weaver, the gay defensive safety. His eyes were staring at my tumescent penis and his jaw was hanging open. "You *are* seeing me," I pointed out to him. I did my best to tuck my equipment back inside my shorts. No offense to gays anywhere, but it's not smart to dangle a bone in front of a wolf.

"I mean privately."

"I don't swing that way, Bubba." No point in leading him on.

"Then there's no problem, Mr. Victor. See, you don't appeal to me, anyway."

I had a flash feeling of rejection but dismissed it immediately lest my manhood be imperiled. Straights like me, it seems, may have a few things to learn from gays. "We can't go to my room for privacy," I told him, understating. "My roommate's in."

"Mine's out. Come on. It's just down the hall."
Bubba led the way.

"What's up?" I asked when he'd closed the door
to his room behind us and we were alone.

"I figure I owe you a favor, Mr. Victor, because
you fixed it so I didn't have to room with Terry and
be tempted by heterosexuality."

"Forget it, Bubba. It was my pleasure," I told
him quite accurately.

"Well, I'm grateful. And I figure it's only right I
repay you."

"Repay me how?"

"I know something I think you might want to
know."

"Oh? About what?"

"About the disappearance of Terry Niemath."

"Go on." Bubba had my full attention now.

"Well, Terry didn't just take off on her own. She
was snatched."

"What do you mean 'snatched'?"

"Taken away. I saw it. Right after the game.
Terry went into Doc Fink's infirmary behind the
locker room. I wanted to see Doc myself because I
had this sprained thumb. But I didn't want to go in
while Terry was there. See, ever since you got me
out of rooming with her, Mr. Victor, Terry would
tease me. I mean she'd make remarks and she'd
wiggle and that kind of thing. So I sort of hung
back to wait until Doc was through with her. Where
I was, I could see through that glass partition to the
infirmary, but I couldn't hear what they were
saying."

"What did you see?"

"First Doc seemed to tell Terry something that upset her. She kept shaking her head 'no' as if to deny what he was telling her, and Doc kept nodding 'yes' like he was telling her it was so true. She seemed to get more and more upset. Finally, he had her roll up the sleeve to her jersey and he gave her a shot."

"A shot? What for?"

"I don't really know. Because she was upset, I guess."

"But he didn't force her to take it, or anything like that?"

"No. From what I could see, she went along with it without any fuss."

"I don't suppose you could see what was in the hypo?"

"No. But, whatever it was, it must have been plenty powerful."

"Why do you say that?"

"Because Terry went out like a light. She just sort of keeled over and curled up on the floor like she was going to sleep. But it must have been a pretty deep sleep, because she didn't move a muscle when they came to take her away."

"When *who* came to take her away?"

"I don't know who," Bubba told me. "All I know is, Doc unlatched the door that leads out to the lot behind the stadium, and these two gorillas came in and carted Terry out like she was a sack of oats. Like I said, she never even twitched when they took her."

"Why didn't you try to stop them?"

"They had guns sticking in their belts. I'm not

that heroic."

"How come you didn't tell Coach Newtrokni about this when there was all the guesswork going on about Terry's disappearing?"

Bubba took a long count before he answered. "I guess I wasn't sure whether or not he was in on it," he said finally in a low voice.

Now it was my turn to think before I spoke. "How come you're so sure about me?" was what I said after the extended pause.

"I'm not." Bubba shrugged. "I just took a chance. Like I said before, it was because you did me that favor."

So I thanked him for the favor. It was obvious from his attitude that Bubba didn't want to get any more deeply involved than that. If there had been any doubt about that, it was banished by the way he clammed up when his roommate entered.

Bubba's roommate was Rhino Dubrowski. He looked happy to find me there. He had tried to get over his hang-ups, but the truth was that Rhino was always a little on edge when he found himself alone with Bubba. He felt this way even though they'd been rooming together all season and Bubba had never so much as winked at him. So, Rhino was glad I was there.

"Come on downstairs, and I'll buy you a drink, old buddy," I suggested.

Rhino's face lit up. Now, he was gladder. He trotted right along with me to the hotel bar.

When he'd slowed down enough over his second bourbon so that I was sure I had his full attention, I told Rhino what Bubba had told me about Terry's being snatched. "Doc Fink slipped her a knockout needle and then turned her over to two cohabitating goons," he summed up. "Well, I think we should have a talk with Doc Fink, Steve."

"I was thinking the same thing myself. The trouble is that he probably won't want to talk to us. Particularly if he's part of a plot to snatch Terry."

"Then I guess we'll have to insist." Rhino shifted his bulk on the barstool; muscles rippled menacingly. "There are ways to make feces talk." Rhino's lip curled, showing fang.

"What do you mean?"

"There are things I learned in intercourse-ing 'Nam!"

"You mean, torture him?" There was shock in my voice.

"'Nam wasn't always pretty." Rhino lapped up another bourbon-and-beer.

"What the hell are you talking about, Rhino? You were a Marine, not a Green Beret."

"I kept my eyes open."

"You were a goddam embassy guard, for Christ's sake! You never even met a Cong any closer than rifle range!"

"Fecal matter! That's no way to talk to me, Steve! Hades! I saved your life!

"Sure you did. And I'm grateful, too. You're a brave man. But you weren't ever any torturer that I know about."

"I saw things!" Rhino insisted mysteriously.

"Okay." I gave up. "Okay. So, you were the Torquemada of Saigon. So, get your fingernail-pullers and your thumbscrew and your rack and your

Chinese water-torture device and let's go pay a call on Doc Fink. Only I'm warning you, Rhino. I can't stand the sight of pain. If you make him suffer too much, I'll go to pieces."

"So don't look, you old, yellow illegitimate child!"

We made our move the next day. We waited until the team was out on the field practicing and then we cornered Doc Fink in his infirmary. Before he knew what was happening, I'd thrown a sack over his head, and Rhino was carting him down to the clubhouse cellar, where we could interrogate him without worrying about being seen or overheard.

"What's the meaning of this?" Those were Doc's first words when we removed the sack. He was a small man with a bristly moustache too imposing for his skinny face. Although he sputtered well, indignation made him ludicrous. "What do you two jokers think you're doing?"

"Never mind that, feces-face!" Rhino raised one hamlike hand threateningly. "We'll ask the questions."

"Are you threatening me?" Doc Fink was quick to pick up on things.

"Darn straight!" Rhino glowered.

Doc thought about it. "I don't get it," he said finally. "What is it you want from me?"

"We want to know about Terry Niemath!"

"I don't know what you're talking about." But his face gave him away.

"You're a lousy liar, Doc," I told him. "We know you gave Terry a shot to knock her out and

210

then turned her over to a couple of strongarm men. Now we want to know why you did it. Who's behind it? Where did they take Terry Niemath?"

"I don't know what you're talking about." It was even less convincing than the first time he'd said it.

"Think again." Rhino lifted him from the chair by his earlobe.

"Violence won't intimidate me!"

"You think he means that?" Rhino grinned ferociously.

"Let's find out."

Rhino propped a thick wooden stave against the wall and broke it in two with a karate chop. He picked up a steel poker and bent it like a pretzel with his bare hands. He lit the stub of a cigar, puffed on it until it was red-hot, and then swallowed it, glowing ash and all.

"I'm not scared!" First impressions are misleading. Doc Fink was obviously a lot tougher than he looked.

"The thumbscrew," I suggested, playing along with Rhino.

"Nothing compared to the est sessions I've been through," Doc countered smugly.

"I'll get the whips," I threatened.

"It won't work. I've had primal therapy. I'm all screamed out."

"The Chinese water-torture."

"No chance. I'm into TM, too. I'll just recite my mantra and ignore it."

"This calls for extreme measures," Rhino realized. "This offspring of a female canine is tough."

I looked at him pleadingly. Tough as I might have talked in an effort to scare information out of Doc Fink, I really wasn't into torture. Basic morality, or something.

"They've got Terry," Rhino reminded me gently. "There's no telling what they're doing to her. We have to fight fire with fire."

"Watch him. I'll be right back."

"Where are you going?"

"There are some things the toughest illegitimate child can't stand up to." And with that he left.

The waiting should have made Doc Fink sweat. It didn't. When Rhino returned he was still cool as a refrigerated cuke. He was curious though. "What's that stuff?" He referred to the items Rhino had lugged back with him.

"What's it look like?"

"A TV set."

"You're a smart illegitimate son."

"But what's that?"

"A video cassette player, you phallus!"

"Then that's a cassette."

"You got it."

"But what's it a cassette of?" Doc Fink wanted to know.

"You're gonna find out." Rhino turned to me. "Help me tie him to this chair, Steve."

"You're going to torture him with that stuff?" I was bewildered.

"Just help me tie him."

I helped Rhino tie Dr. Fink to the chair. When he was secured, Rhino set up the TV set and the video cassette player in front of him. Then he stuck

212

a gag in Doc Fink's mouth. "So nobody hears his screams," he explained. He plugged earphones into the TV and put them on Doc Fink. Last of all, he plugged in the cassette.

The cassette was a replay of the last Monday night football game the Stonewalls had played against the Miami Dolphins. It had been a pretty good game, fast-moving, packed with action, the score seesawing back and forth.

Watching it, I wondered what Rhino could possibly be up to. After all, Doc Fink was looking at the same replay I was. The only difference was that I couldn't hear the sound and he could. But why should that make any difference? Why should that make him crack and tell us what we wanted to know?

It seemed ridiculous, and yet his screams, muffled by the gag, began before the first quarter was even over. Rhino let him suffer a little before he removed the gag. "Ready to talk?" he asked.

"No! I'll never talk! Never!"

Rhino replaced the gag and the earphones. By halftime, tears were streaming down Doc's face. "Please! Please!" he begged when Rhino removed the gag again.

"Who's behind the snatching of Terry Niemath?"

"I don't know! I swear, I don't know! Please! Don't make me—"

But Rhino was merciless. He replaced the gag and the earphones once again. The Stonewall-Dolphin game proceeded.

The next time he removed Doc Fink's gag, there

was no doubt that Rhino's technique had worked. "I'll talk!" he babbled. "I'll talk! I'll tell you anything you want to know! Just turn it off! Please! Please! Turn it off! I'll talk!"

"Who set up Terry Niemath?"

"The Baroquians! Somebody named Putnam. He paid me to knock her out so his men could snatch her. The Baroquians kidnapped her!"

The Baroquians! I was floored. I'd figured the mob, maybe, trying to narrow the point spread. But the Baroquians? Charles Putnam? Why would they kidnap Terry Niemath?

"Why?" Rhino demanded of Doc Fink. "Why'd they do it?"

"I don't know! I swear I don't know! I'd tell you if I knew! Don't torture me any more! I would! I swear it! Just don't make me listen to Howard Cosell announcing any more! Have mercy! No more Howard Cosell!"

Howard Cosell! That's torture!

CHAPTER ELEVEN

"Shut up, Howard!" Doc Fink was still babbling from the results of the Cosell torture. "I want to know who tackled who! Shut up, Howard! I don't care that the home city of the Stonewalls was named after the poet John Greenleaf Whittier! Shut up, Howard! I want to know if the pass was called back or not! I already know that the Watergate wimp played football for four years at Whittier College and could never make the first team. Shut up, Howard! I want to know if they made the first down or if they were short, not how the incumbent was shafted in Whittier's Twelfth Congressional District in 1956. Shut up, Howard! Shut up! Shut up! Shut up!"

"Get hold of yourself, man." Rhino slapped him lightly back and forth across the face to cut off his hysteria.

"Sorry." Doc Fink calmed down to a shudder.

"It was just so awful!"

"Lots of people watch Monday Night Football," I reminded him. "Millions of TV fans listen to Howard Cosell."

"But not without commercials," Doc Fink reminded me. "You have no idea how horrible it can be uninterrupted."

"Where did they take Terry Niemath?" I got back to the business at hand.

"They'll kill me if I tell you."

"It's either that or more Cosell."

"Some place they called 'the Orchard'. That's all I know."

"The Baroquian Orchard?"

"They just called it 'the Orchard'."

I turned to Rhino. "Let's go."

That afternoon, on the plane to San Francisco, Rhino explained to me where he'd gotten the idea for using the Cosell cassettes to torture the truth out of Doc Fink. "There's this bar up near Buffalo I read about in the papers. The owner bought up a hundred used twelve-inch black-and-white TV sets at scrap prices. On Monday nights he'd turn 'em to Cosell one at a time. For twenty bucks, a customer could kick in a TV set when Howard started talking. In three weeks, the guy had tripled his business. The only trouble was that, by that time, he'd run out of sets. They'd all been kicked in by Cosell-tortured fans. Isn't that a urinator?"

"Perfectly understandable."

We fell silent as the stewardess brought us our drinks. When she'd departed, I turned to Rhino

216

once again. "I think we'd better talk about what we're doing," I suggested. "Has it occurred to you that we work for Charles Putnam and his group of Baroquians? They're the ones who hired us to put Terry Niemath across as a quarterback in the first place. And now it looks like they're the ones who grabbed her. I think, before we actually do anything about getting her back, we're going to have to decide exactly where we stand."

"My first cohabitating obligation is to the Whittier Stonewalls," Rhino answered. "I'm a scout for them."

"Suppose the Putnam group, finding out Terry was pregnant, decided the best thing for the team would be to have her vanish?"

"You think that's what happened?"

"I don't know. I guess it's one of the things we're on our way to San Francisco to find out."

"What if they had another reason for snatching her? Are we going to try to get her back?"

"That, old buddy, is the question," I told him.

"What do we do first?"

"Get a good night's sleep after we land. Rent a car in the morning. Drive out to the Baroquian Orchard and case the situation. Depending on what we find out, we'll decide then what to do."

"In other words, we get our feces together and play it by ear."

"You got it."

It was mid-morning when we reached the access road to the Baroquian Orchard the next day and were forced to make our first decision. Since we weren't expected, there was a good chance that, if we drove up the road to the guard booth, we would be turned away. So we stashed the car behind a clump of bushes at the foot of the road and set out on foot.

We did not, however, set out empty-handed. Remembering the chain-link fence which surrounded the Baroquian's property, we had thought to buy a pair of stout wirecutters in San Francisco, and now we took them with us. Emerging from a grove of redwoods which reduced us to ant height, we faced a remote stretch of this fence with no guards in sight. In a matter of minutes we had cut enough of it away to pass through to the other side.

It was straight uphill from there through a tangle of underbrush that crackled like breakfast cereal. Was it any wonder that we attracted the attention of one of the guards who patrolled the Baroquian Orchard? Fortunately for us, this particular sentinel wasn't very long on imagination. He jumped me without bothering to determine if there was more than one of us. Rhino plucked him off me with no more trouble than if he'd been a tick on a spaniel's ear.

"What should we do with the maternal mater?" Rhino dangled him by his uniform collar.

"Possession is nine-tenths of the law," I told him. "You decide."

Rhino decided to relieve him of his underpants and pants and hang him upside down from an oak tree branch. Bound, gagged, and half-naked, the guard presented a sight that would have the mountain forest animals chattering among themselves for days. Rhino patted his cheek and we continued on our upward trek.

A quarter of a mile or so later, we struck a path and, a little while after that, the terrain leveled out, and we found ourselves just behind the ninth hole of the Baroquian golf course. As we were getting our bearings, a golf ball fell from the sky and bounced off poor Rhino's skull. A half-minute later there was a jovial shout: "FORE!"

Rhino was just coming around when the man who had shouted stumbled on us. He was driving a golf cart and chewing gum. He braked to a halt when he saw Rhino stretched out on the ground. "Good Lord!" he exclaimed. "What happened?"

"I was hit by a cohabitating golf ball!" Rhino told him groggily.

"But I yelled 'FORE!' "

"You're supposed to yell before you hit the ball." I recognized him as one of the ex-Presidents of the U.S. we had encountered on our last visit to the Baroquian Club.

"Really? I didn't know that. You see, I'm new to the game. Football and skiing have always been my sports."

"You look familiar." Rhino's eyes began to focus.

"Gosh, thanks. I don't get recognized too much any more. Not like when I was President."

"Of course!" Rhino snapped his fingers. "You were President of the United States."

"Not for long." There was a wistful note in his voice. "None of us seem to last in office as long as Presidents used to last. Maybe that's why there's so many of us ex-Presidents wandering around."

"How's it feel?" I asked Rhino.

"Sore as a boil on a phallus."

"I feel just awful," the ex-President confided. "It's all my fault. Is there anything I can do for you?" he asked Rhino. "What would make it feel better?"

"You wouldn't have a shot of bourbon with you?"

"No. I'm afraid not. Wait a minute." He snapped his fingers, almost catching his ear-lobe between them. "We can get you a drink at the main building. Perhaps I could even buy you gentlemen lunch to make up for my carelessness." There was a wistful note in his voice as though he wasn't often successful in enticing someone to have lunch with him since leaving the White House. "Just get in the golf cart with me and I'll drive us there in a jiffy."

His jiffy was about five minutes at a thrill a minute, the way he drove. Hanging on for dear life, I tried to think about our situation. Since we were now guests of the ex-President, nobody would question our right to be in the building. We'd be okay as long as we didn't run into anyone who might remember us from our last visit. Even then, we'd probably go unchallenged unless the somebody was Putnam or someone else who was in on the snatching of Terry Niemath and who was also aware that we weren't privy to the latest game plan.

And so, we sailed into the Baroquian mansion as his guests with no questions asked. After a somewhat boring lunch of some dish that was both fishy and creamed—my two pet hates—an upper-level Exxon executive, fully bearded, skipped through the dining lounge dressed in a miniskirt and tube-top. "Hi there!" He waved flirtatiously at the ex-Prez.

"Oh, hi there, Chip. What's up?"

"Rehearsal. I'm late. Gotta run." He bounced off.

"Oh, the show!" The ex-Prez snapped his fingers again, just managing to miss his nose. "Gee whiz. I forgot all about it. Would you fellows like to watch them rehearse?"

Rhino and I exchanged glances. We had no better plan for how to proceed. We went along with the ex-Prez to watch the Baroquians rehearse their show.

They were in the middle when we entered and took seats in the back of the hall. There seemed to be a good deal of confusion. Men in a variety of female garb—some half-in and half-out of costume—were limbering up and rehearsing dance steps without regard to the turmoil around them. A choreographer was trying to plot out a dance routine with a quartet of burly, cigar-chomping cabinet officers in tinkerbell costumes. A corporation president in a pulled-up evening gown sat with his legs propped up against the back of a scenery flat so that he could shave them with an electric razor. Another mogul was struggling with a lipstick and a hand-mirror. The overall scene looked like a cross between Guccione's *Caligula* and *Where's Charley?*

A former Secretary of State appeared with a former National Security Advisor, who hadn't quite made it to Secretary of State, at his side. He called for order. Both the call and his accent were echoed by the other man. They were evidently the director and assistant director of the show. Their combined Germanic persona quieted things down.

"That Henry!" the ex-Prez whispered worshipfully at my side. "He sure knows how to make them listen!" He popped his gum.

"We vill take ze Havaiian number right from ze top," he instructed. "Everybody else, off ze stage. *Mach schnell!*"

A semblance of order appeared onstage. A group of male chorines wearing grass skirts and leis arranged themselves in a line. They were made up with Man-tan, and some kind of eye make-up had been used to try to angle the corners of their eyes in what someone had conceived to be an Oriental slant. Now they began to dance a hula and sing to an accompaniment of mandolins playing *Wicki Wacki Woo.* Half of them had shaved their legs; the other half looked like tree trunks with caterpillar blight. They were about as graceful as a herd of hippopotami splashing around the waterhole.

"The boys are pretty talented, aren't they?" the ex-Prez whispered to me.

"Sure are," I lied.

"I always envy them that. I've got two left feet myself."

The chorus line could have used two more left feet, but I didn't tell him that. He should have been able to see it for himself. Henry was stamping on the floor like a drill sergeant in an effort to introduce the errant ones to the beat of the music.

They stamped back, but the tempo still eluded them.

The chorus line receded toward the back of the stage, fading toward the wings on either side. A spotlight created a diffused and amber puddle in the empty space between the two halves of the line. A new figure—tall, curvy, sinuous—appeared in a sarong dating back to Dorothy Lamour. The chorus subsided to a supporting role as this 'star' performed a hula-style tap dance and sang the lyric to *Wicki Wacki Woo.*

I blinked and did a double-take. Beside me, Rhino's jaw fell open as though the hinge had just rusted away. Despite the long black *wahine* wig, there could be no doubting the identity of the newcomer. It was Terry Niemath!

"Isn't he great?" The ex-President was admiring.

"He's sensational." I went along with the gender. "Who is he?"

"New fellow. A real find. I mean, you talk about talent! Just look at that chest!"

"Nice legs too," I agreed.

"You betcha. If I didn't know it was a man impersonating a woman, I'd think it was the real thing."

"He could have fooled me," said Rhino.

"When the number's over, do you think you could introduce us to him?" I asked the ex-Prez.

"Golly, I don't know. I haven't really met him myself. He's new. A friend of Charlie Putnam's, I believe."

"I see."

The number wound down to a bump-and-grind finale. It may not have been authentic hula, but it was effective. The ex-Prez was still applauding enthusiastically when the assistant director and former National Security Advisor held up his hands for silence. "It iss two-thirty," he announced when he had everybody's attention.

Audience and cast stood up as one and started for the various exits.

"What's up?" I detained the ex-Prez with a hand on his arm.

"It's two-thirty," he explained.

"So?"

"Piss call." A passing wood nymph with five o'clock shadow paused to explain.

I looked blank.

"Tradition," the wood nymph elucidated, scratching his stubble. "Every day at two thirty, we Baroquians go outside and empty our bladders against the trunks of the redwood trees. You fellows must be guests, or you would have known that. You should have told them," he chastised the ex-Prez.

"Gee, I forgot." He was on his feet and moving towards the exits with the other men.

"Suppose you don't have the need?" I inquired.

"It's tradition!" the wood nymph told me in an injured tone of voice. "You can't go against tradition."

"Like not letting women join or work at the club?"

"Sure. We couldn't relieve ourselves against the trees if there were women around, could we? I mean, how would that look?"

"A lot of women are probably wondering about that very thing right now."

"Gosh, do you really think so? I mean, I didn't think that ladies—" The ex-Prez was troubled.

"I was only kidding."

"Oh. Ha ha." The ex-Prez laughed politely. "Well, I have to go."

"When you gotta go, you gotta go."

"What about you fellows? The tradition includes guests, you know." The wood nymph was concerned.

"We'll be along in a minute."

"Don't be late. We try to do it all together. In the spirit of good fellowship, you know. We call it the 'unit rule'."

"Right behind you," I assured him, lying in my teeth.

The hall emptied out quickly. Soon the only ones left were Rhino and myself and the hula skirted 'star' up on the stage. We approached her.

"Steve!" She sprang to her feet as she recognized us. "Rhino! What are you-all doin' here?"

"Looking for you," I told her. "The question is what are you doing here dancing a hula with a bunch of honchos in drag when the Superbowl is only a week away?"

"Seems I got me a problem, Steve." Terry hung her head. "Bun in the oven."

"We know all about your problem. But what are you doing here?"

"I done passed out in Doc Fink's office 'count of my condition. No way I could be playin' them practice scrimmages now that I'm in the family way. I mean, I'd surely lose the little bugger. So they brought me here to the Baroquian Orchard for my own sake."

"Did it occur to you that the shot Doc gave you might have had something to do with your passing out?"

"Nope." Terry looked bewildered. "Why would I thank a thang like that?"

"Because you were shanghaied," I told her. "As far as the team is concerned, you just vanished."

"Why, that Mister Putnam said as how he'd explain it to you-all, an' there wouldn't be any problem a-tall."

"That wasn't done, Terry. What else did he tell you?" I wondered.

"He explained as how it would be immoral to get an abortion."

"I'll bet!" Charles Putnam, champion of the all-male exclusivity practiced at the Baroquian Club, would of course have had the last word on morality for women! "Do you have any idea who the father is?" I asked Terry.

"Why yes, I do declare I thank I do."

"Do you think it's me, Terry?" I faced up to the responsibility squarely.

"Why, Steve darlin', next thang you'll be offerin' to make an honest woman outa me. No, sugah, I surely do not believe it's your doin'. I was always careful to use my diaphragm with us."

"Somebody else on the team?"

"Not our team. No. I was always protected."

"Who then?"

"Way back, early on in the season, there was this

226

pile-up in one of the games. One of the opposing tackles—I'm still not sure which one—he put it to me there under the mess of bodies."

"Are you trying to tell me that he had sex with you right on the field?"

"I do believe so."

"But—But—"

"I never did put in my diaphragm *before* the games. Didn't rightly seem to be any need."

"I should think not!"

"Never figured it would come up during a game."

"Not with the TV cameras and all," I agreed. "But listen, Terry." I shook my head disbelievingly. "The time element—?"

"Well now, whoever this fellow was, he had some mighty fast moves. I'm not denyin' that. Slid down my pants. Put it in. Came. Pulled out. Pulled up my pants. It was all over by the time the referee blew his whistle."

"But what about you?"

"Tell the truth, I didn't have me no orgasm, Steve. Now, that surely doesn't happen to me too often."

"That's not what I mean. What I mean is, why didn't you say something?"

"You mean like to the referee? Or the line judge? Didn't hardly seem worth makin' a fuss, Steve. I mean, suppose they penalized him ten yards for illegal procedure? Why, I'd just have had to turn down the penalty. You see, I'd just completed a pass for a first down before they piled onto me."

"Are you sure that was when you got pregnant?"

"That's the only time it could have been." Terry sighed. "Sure wasn't much fun for so much trouble."

"Mr. Victor!" The voice came from the other end of the hall—cold, commanding, and familiar. "What are you doing here?" Charles Putnam demanded. He strode towards us, an imposing authoritative figure.

"Rescuing Terry Niemath." I refused to be intimidated. "The question is, what's she doing here?"

"That doesn't concern you."

"The hell it doesn't."

"You are in our employ, Mr. Victor. Hired to do our bidding. You and Mr. Dubrowski. I recall no orders summoning you here. Nor is Miss Niemath in need of rescuing. She is being looked after very well, thank you."

"What about the Superbowl?" Rhino blurted out.

"Due to circumstances which needn't concern you, she will not be playing in the Superbowl."

"They already know 'bout my delicate condition," Terry informed him.

"I see." Putnam nodded. "Then no further explanation is needed. You two will return to your duties with the team. Miss Niemath will remain here with us."

"It won't wash, Putnam. It's not just her being pregnant. There's something very fishy going on here."

"Nonsense!" You are being unnecessarily

228

melodramatic, Mr. Victor. I can't imagine why you should think there is anything more to this than the obvious embarrassment to the team of a quarterback who is—as the French say—*enceinte*."

"I think there's more to it," I said carefully, "because you wouldn't allow a female on these sacrosanct male premises unless there was some really overriding reason."

"Don't be naive, Mr. Victor. Certain females have graced these premises on other occasions. We are men, after all. Our needs are the needs of the masculine gender."

"I'm not talking about the tootsies for your stag parties and you know it. I'm talking about a woman that's not here for your pleasure, a woman who sees you in your tutus, a woman who might even see you watering the redwoods, a woman so important to you that you even pass her off as a man impersonating a female and stick her in one of your silly shows."

"Oh, Steve, but that's such downright fun!" Terry exclaimed.

"You've sucked me in, Mr. Putnam." I ignored her. "I don't know into what, but I'm going to find out. There's more involved here than Terry's condition, and I want to know what it is. What's more, Mr. Putnam, you're going to tell me."

"I don't think so, Mr. Victor. I think that what I am going to do is discharge you. Mr. Victor, you are fired."

"Mr. Putnam." Rhino spoke up. "If you fire Steve, I quit."

"So be it." Putnam's haughtiness reached its

peak. "You two will be so good as to leave the Baroquian premises immediately. If you delay, I shall have you removed."

"It won't wash," I told him. "Not only won't we leave, but if you don't tell me what the hell is going on, we're going straight to the newspapers and tell them everything that's happened so far, including how you shot Terry up with a loaded hypo so you could kidnap her and bring her here."

Putnam looked at me for a long moment and then sighed. "I had forgotten just how obnoxiously persistent you can be, Mr. Victor." His voice was no warmer, but there was a note of resignation in it. "Very well. It seems you have me over a barrel. I will tell you the truth and throw myself and my Baroquian associates on your mercy."

"Get out the handkerchiefs," I advised Rhino, trusting Putnam no more than ever.

" 'Scuse me." Terry interrupted us. "I have to go to the necessary. I'll be back soon as I finish my business." She left.

"Are you going to listen to me, Mr. Victor? Or are you going to make wisecracks?" Charles Putnam wanted to know after she had gone.

"I'm going to listen," I replied. "Shoot."

"Very well. Now, you may remember, Mr. Victor, that on the occasion of our first telephone conversation regarding the Whittier Stonewalls I described how our little group had enfranchised the team as a tribute to the most famous malefactor of modern American politics."

"You didn't describe him that way back then."

"Exactly. I was, I suppose, sugar-coating the truth."

230

"You don't mean that you lied to me, Mr. Putnam?" I mocked him. "I can't believe that."

"Not exactly. I sugar-coated the truth," he insisted. "It is true that the team was set up to honor this man. It is true that we paid for it. It is not true, however, that we did so voluntarily. The fact is, we were forced into doing it."

"Forced how?"

"The gentleman in question had come into possession of certain files compiled by a long-time head of the FBI, since deceased. These files contained certain unsavory information relating to each member of our little group."

"Surely not you too, Mr. Putnam."

"We are all of us vulnerable, Mr. Victor. I can only tell you that my own not inconsiderable files would have been enough to have silenced the original compiler, had he but lived."

"But not enough to keep the whiz of Whittier off your back? You didn't have anything on him?"

"Considerable. Enough, believe me, to have deterred a more savory man. But what is there one can threaten to reveal about him that could compare with what is already known? Alas, Mr. Victor, his threat had more weight than any counterthreat might have had for the simple reason that we are all vulnerable, whereas disgrace has placed his reputation beyond threat."

"So, he blackmailed you into setting up the team, and you went along with it. Go on."

"Blackmail is an ugly word, Mr. Victor. He did, however, persuade us against our will."

"Call it what you will, it pissed you off."

231

"We are not the type of men who get angry, Mr. Victor. We are the type of men who get even."

"And getting even has something to do with snatching Terry."

"Her pregnancy did indeed provide us with an opportunity to avenge ourselves. But timing, as you know, is everything. We do not want her condition known until the last possible moment. We do not even want it known that she has disappeared. You have a ringer, and that is working out. All I ask, Mr. Victor, is that you let us decide when to reveal the truth."

"And all this is to get even?"

"Yes."

"Is he betting heavily on the Stonewalls? Is that it?"

"In a manner of speaking."

I thought about that. I had a flash of insight. "The stock market!" I exclaimed. "It always shoots up or down depending on whether an original AFL or NFL team wins the Superbowl. That's it, isn't it? He's shifted his stock market holdings because he thinks the Stonewalls will win with Terry at quarterback. He's in deep, and you're letting him get in deeper. You're trying to ruin him completely!"

"It's no more than he deserves." Putnam confirmed my deduction in a soft tone of voice. "And we're not really doing anything so wrong. We're only delaying the inevitable revelation. Terry Niemath wouldn't be able to play in any case. After all, she is pregnant."

"Y'all hold on there a minute!" Terry had returned and stood now in the doorway to the rehearsal hall with her hands on her hips. "That there doctor made a real bad mistake with that test. I just got my monthlies!"

"What did you say?" I was startled.

"I thank Doc Fink was put up to lyin' to me. I ain't pregnant no more. Ask me, I never was!"

I stared at Terry. She wasn't pregnant. The Whittier Stonewalls quarterback wasn't pregnant.

Terry Niemath could play in the Superbowl!

CHAPTER TWELVE

Superbowl Sunday! The television was on and I was already guzzling the first cold brew. In the bed beside me, Stephanie Greenwillow was warm and willing. Whittier kicked off to the Philadelphia Eagles. Stephanie stroked my balls. All was right with my world. But not quite . . .

"I'm still mixed up." Stephanie's voice drowned out announcer Engberg. "Why would Doc Fink tell Terry she was pregnant when she wasn't?"

"So she wouldn't make any fuss when she woke up at the Baroquian Orchard and realized she was missing practice for the Superbowl." Distracted, I didn't see the Philly runback.

"And Doc was working for this Charles Putnam and his Baroquian friends?"

"Yeah." Montgomery picked up three yards.

"So he lied to the coach."

"Yeah."

234

"And Coach Newtrokni didn't know anything about all this?"

"That's right." Jaworski's first pass went incomplete.

"I see." Stephanie kissed me. Her lips were soft, damp, parted. Her mouth was warm, inviting. Her tongue was teasing, clever. It was a long kiss. I missed the next play entirely. When I opened my eyes, it was to find that Philly, short of the first down, was punting.

"So what it really adds up to—" Stephanie resumed talking, "—is that Putnam and the others built Terry and the team up all the way to the Superbowl just so they could yank the rug out from under Terry to make the Stonewalls lose." Indignant, she popped up to her knees at the foot of the bed with her hands on her hips. Her red hair, cropped when she had been standing in for Terry, was like a fiery halo surrounding the anger in her face. Her high, round breasts heaved emotionally under the black silk of the nightgown she was wearing, their creamy top halves rising out of and then sinking into the bodice. The flare of her generous hips from her narrow waist blocked the TV set. This time I missed the Stonewalls' runback and their first play.

"That's what it adds up to." I sat up and reached out to put my hands on Terry's hips to move her so that I could see the screen.

She misunderstood and slid over me. Sharp nipples bit through the silk and into my naked chest as she lay over me. The warmth of her thighs blanketed mine. I stroked her warm, plump, jutting

235

bottom as we kissed again. It was another long kiss and throughout it her body moved slowly and invitingly over mine. My penis began to rise between her squirming thighs. My next look at the TV set over Stephanie's round shoulder showed me that the Eagles had regained possession of the ball. I never did find out how.

Sensing my distraction, Stephanie rolled off me and sat up again. "And they put that poor girl through all that trauma—drugging her, telling her she was pregnant, convincing her not to have an abortion—they did all that just so they could get even with that man for blackmailing them into buying him a football team in the first place!"

"Yeah . . . Steph, you're blocking the set again."

"Well, you know what I think?" She ignored my complaint.

"No. What do you think?"

"I think they're childish."

"Okay."

"I mean, these are big important men, the men who run the country, the world. And look how they behave! Petty! Childish!" she railed. "But you know what really gets me?"

"No. What?" I gave up on the first quarter. From what little I could gather, it was pretty seesaw anyway, and neither team seemed able to get within scoring distance.

"The rest of us let them do it! They're schoolboys playing silly games with grudge matches and all kinds of kid manipulations, and they're running the world the same way, and the rest of us let them do it!"

"I guess you're right." I really didn't want to argue with her. I wanted to watch the Superbowl, drink my beer, and maybe fool around a little during the time-outs. Was that so much to ask?

"They run an automobile company and get petulant when it turns out that they're not selling cars because the Japanese are building small ones, and they're building big gas-eaters, and the public prefers the little ones—something any man on the street could have predicted—and then we taxpayers have to give them money so they can stay in business. What do you call that?"

"It's called free enterprise," I told her in a neutral voice.

"That's not what I call it! I call it a government handout!" Her green eyes sparkled with fury.

"You're gorgeous when you're angry." I reached out with the middle fingers of both hands and stroked the nipples of her breasts through the black silk. I wanted to calm her down; sex or football, one or the other, but please get off the soapbox.

She purred. She took the two long fingers in her hands. She kissed their tips. Then she replaced them over her now erect nipples.

"... and so at the start of the second quarter it's still a scoreless game ..." I heard Olsen announcing.

Again Stephanie reacted to my being distracted, withdrawing the pulsing, long tips of her quivering breasts from my touch. "Or we put them in charge of armies and massive weapons systems and they move them around like toy soldiers and battery-operated doohickeys you give kids for Christmas.

They shake their toy swords and go all red in the face and start yelling that our father can beat up their father, and what they're talking about is nuclear war! What do you call that?"

"Maintaining an arms balance for peace," I suggested. "And don't be strident. It makes your face go all red."

"Strident!" Her voice wasn't strident as she said it; it was shrill. "You mean I should walk softly and carry a big neutron bomb like these men in their tutus do?"

"Make love, not war," I suggested, falling back on an old saw. I sat up and drew her into my arms placatingly. Over her shoulder I saw Terry Niemath fading back into the slot and firing off a long pass. Kiss number three prevented me from seeing if it was completed.

Stephanie came to me willingly enough. She was all churned up with resentment and it worked on her libido. Anger, I've noticed frequently, has that effect on some women and some men as well. It makes them horny.

Her being horny made me horny too. Stephanie looked particularly delectable with the black silk clinging to her voluptuous body from bosom to knee. I pushed down one of the thin straps over her shoulder and bared one of her firm, melon-shaped breasts. The aroused nipple quivered in its center like a small lipstick. I bent and licked it with the very tip of my tongue.

"Ahh!" She moaned and her slender, graceful fingers tangled in my hair. "Ohh, Steve! You bastard! You know how sensitive my nipples are!"

238

I drew the nipple between my lips and bit down on it ever so gently. Her fingers tightened over the base of my neck. Holding the breast-tip that way, softly but firmly between my teeth, I proceeded to lick it rhythmically with the full length of my tongue. It was like running a swatch of velvet over it. Stephanie shivered and clutched me to her even more closely.

"... and it looks like it's going to be a long one ..." Engberg's voice rose excitedly from the TV set. *A long one? Who? Which side? Was it complete?* Stephanie bent and licked the inside of my ear and I heard no more.

Her tongue in my ear spoke, blotting out whatever there might have been to hear. "Suck harder!" Her voice was husky. "Take more of my breast in your mouth. More!"

I drew the firm white flesh into my mouth and sucked with my lips. Panting and squirming, Stephanie clawed my shoulders with her nails. We were both in sitting positions on the bed now, me with my head bent to her bared breast, her with her tantalizing mouth nuzzling and licking and nibbling at my ear.

Dropping my hands, I reached under her nightie to caress her thighs. Shapely and sleek, they burned under my touch. Moaning again, she stretched her legs straight out in front of her, over the edge of the bed. Stephanie would loathe the description, but they are truly chorus girl legs. Their lightly-muscled perfection has always been a turn-on for me.

It worked that way now. Looking at Stephanie's

legs with her writhing breast in my mouth, I became aware that under my jockey shorts my stiffening prick was climbing my belly. She noticed too.

"Oh, my!" Her agile tongue made the words a caress in my ear. "You're getting *so* excited!" She turned her outstretched legs this way and that. Then she separated them, widening the space between them, causing her nightie to ride further up her flushed thighs until its hem was almost at the juncture of her insinuatingly twisting limbs. "Do I excite you, Steve? Is that it? Is it me?"

"Damn straight!" I raised my head to find her green eyes smoldering wantonly as they met mine. Holding her gaze, I slipped out of my shorts. Her eyes dropped to the naked erection bristling between my legs. They narrowed to greedy slits of green-gold. Her tongue circled her lips like a snake drawn from its lair by the heat of the sun. She reached down and circled me with her fist. Under her touch my prick jumped with a will of its own. But when I ordered it to subside, it did so, albeit reluctantly. "Yeah!" I told Stephanie. "It sure is you!"

"I see." She wriggled her bottom cunningly on the bed where she was sitting. The result was that the nightie tightened and climbed up higher. Her *mons veneris* was revealed like a choice, copper-colored, particularly succulent fruit. The silky triangle of red hair shimmered as with the dew of her desire. The high mound rose from her body like a small hillock as she leaned back on her elbows. The purple lips had a patina of moist cream and they were parted invitingly. The meatiness between them was throbbing and pink. The deeper red tip of her swollen clitoris was just barely visible. Stephanie lifted her bottom slightly and her pussy opened still more widely. "You can play with it if you like," she suggested.

"I like!" I ran my hands up between her thighs and she lifted still higher. The rosy flesh was slick with a mixture of perspiration and lusting lubrication. I traced the purple lips with my fingertips and Stephanie gasped. Tentatively, I dipped one fingertip. The mouth of her cunt closed around it like a Venus Flytrap capturing its prey.

Stephanie looked down the length of her body to where my hand squirmed between her legs. She laughed excitedly. Her pussy opened slightly and she slid down the length of my finger. Her clitty stroked it as she did so. Then, with a sudden gesture of abandonment, she flung herself backwards on the bed, raised her legs so that they were bent at the knees, and arced them as widely apart as possible. The movement presented her gaping pussy to view like some erotic feast. "I'd really like it if you kissed me there, Steve." Her voice was quavery as she said it.

Three cheers for women's liberation! If nothing else, it has freed up feminine bedmates to ask for what gratifies them. And if there's one thing I've learned as the man from O.R.G.Y., it's that satisfying a woman while making love to her always—always!—makes the man's experience more gratifying.

I slid to the floor on my knees. I put one hand

241

under Stephanie's hot and writhing bottom. I reached my other hand up to her breast and grasped it, palming the long, quivering nipple. Then I bent my head to the treasure between her legs.

Stephanie moaned as I ran my tongue up between her muscle-tensed thighs. I felt her heart speed up wildly as I dipped into her honeyed well. When my lips closed over the swollen, purple lips of her quim in a sucking kiss, she let out a little yelp and raised her bottom to arch her belly so that the pressure there—and the suckling sensation—would be increased.

Continuing to suck her, I explored with my tongue. The inside of her pussy, while coated with syrup, was tightly ridged. When my tongue grazed her clitty, the ridges clutched at my tongue like the fingers of a hand transforming itself into a fist. Deliberately, I broke off contact with the stiff, aroused clitty. Immediately both of Stephanie's fists pummeled my shoulders. I squeezed her nipple and she subsided. I pushed my tongue all the way up inside her and began moving it in and out as if it was a prick fucking her. The lower part of her body began bouncing frantically as if that was the case. The bounces were contrived to rub her clitty over my tongue, but again I avoided the contact. I didn't want Stephanie to come this way. I wanted her to come when my cock was inside her.

"Oh!" she pleaded. "Please! I'm so hot! Please! I can't get any hotter!"

She was wrong. When I slid my hand between the bouncing globes of her behind I found another furnace there and turned up the heat still more. My fingertip playing with her 'quick' while I sucked and licked her pussy made her even more frantic.

"You devil!" Her fists were pounding my shoulders once again. "Suck my clitty! Lick my clitty! Play with it! ... Something! Something! ..." She writhed wildly over my double penetration of her most intimate recesses. "You devil! You devil!"

My cock was sticking out in front of me like a policeman's billy. Stephanie couldn't reach it, but she kept clawing at my belly with the effort. Finally she managed to reach my pubic hair and tugged at it demandingly.

I got to my feet. I pushed Stephanie back on the bed. I lifted her legs over my shoulders. I drew back, ready to plunge, and—

And Stephanie Greenwillow rolled out from under me and off the bed to the floor.

"What the hell—?" I stared down at her, suddenly feeling foolish.

She looked back at me with gold-green eyes that were still cloudy with passion. Her lovely, ripe breasts were still panting, the long nipples still bright red with lust. The swollen lips of her cunt were still squeezing and unsqueezing regularly as if beyond her control. "Let's not hurry things, Steve." Her voice quavered.

"What the hell do you mean 'hurry things'? Unless I'm nuts, we're both as ready to fuck as we'll ever be!"

"What I mean is that I know how important it is to you to watch the Superbowl."

"The Superbowl ..." I echoed blankly. Truthfully, it had gone out of my mind.

"Because of your involvement with the Stonewalls all season," Stephanie explained, "I understand how important this game must be to you."

"Stephanie!" I rallied my senses. "Is this your idea of getting even with me for last year, or what?"

"Not at all," she said. "Really." She certainly looked sincere. "I just think you should watch the game. And besides, we can sort of fool around while you're watching and we'll get so hot ... so hot ..." Her voice trailed off. "It will be fun!" She looked very turned on by the idea.

"My balls will bust!"

"No they won't," she promised. "I'll soothe them. She laid down beside me on the bed, her head on the pillow next to mine. She reached down and cupped my balls in one hand. She stroked them with the fingers of her other hand.

I looked at the TV screen. It was halftime. I had no idea what the score was. "Why don't we just get laid now, real quick, and then relax and watch the second half," I suggested to Stephanie.

"Why, Steve! Neither one of us has ever been much for quickies. Besides, it'll be so-o-o-o much better if we build up to it slowly."

"I'm already built up. And besides, it's halftime. There's no game to watch."

"Well, I didn't finish what I was saying before anyway. There was one more thing I wanted to point out."

"Please, Stephanie! Not politics! Not when I'm

244

in this condition!"

"Your condition is perfectly delightful." She squeezed my inflamed balls fondly. "What I wanted to say about those destructive boys playing their asinine games at the Baroquian Club is that the worst thing we allow them to do is run our governments—city, state, national and world—Democratic and Communist and Third World. We actually give these ninnies who have to exclude women from their clubs so they can urinate on trees—we actually give them the power to make laws to govern us, laws to dump food surpluses while babies go hungry, laws to subsidize nuclear plants they can't control, laws to tell women what they can and can't do with their bodies, laws—"

"Stephanie!" I interrupted desperately. "You're squeezing too hard!"

"Oh! Sorry!" She loosened her grip on my balls.

"Besides," I said quickly before she could resume her diatribe, "the second half is starting."

"Okay." She patted my genitals soothingly and subsided.

I learned now, for the first time, that the first half had ended with the score Eagles 14, Whittier 10. Jaworski, 'the Polish Rifle', had evidently done his homework well enough to pierce the Stonewalls' defense with two long passes that had set up the touchdowns for Philly. The Philly defense, on the other hand, had devoted themselves to a pass-rush blitz that had held Terry Niemath to one touchdown bomb plus a series of buttonhooks mixed with bootlegs that had culminated in a field goal. Coming out for the second half, the

Stonewalls looked grim. They'd gotten out of the habit of being on the short end of the halftime score.

The kickoff was called dead in the Whittier end zone and it was first-and-ten on their own twenty. Stonewalls halfback Luther went around the right side for four yards. On second down, Terry's pass to Pete Gorgonzola was knocked away by left corner-back Roynell Young. On the next play, she connected with a slant-out bullet to tight end Craig Cramp, and Whittier had the first down. As they lined up on the thirty-six, Stephanie nuzzled her head on my chest, being elaborately careful not to block the TV screen, and tongued my left nipple. My semi-hard prick nodded acknowledgement.

On the second play, Terry Niemath threw a long one straight down the middle. This time Gorgonzola got under it and held on. Two plays later, Luther went over for the TD. Horseshoe Cohen kicked the extra point, and Whittier was ahead seventeen to fourteen.

"Go, team!" I exclaimed jubilantly. Stephanie, reacting, ran her tongue down from my chest to my belly. When I shivered, she laughed a low, throaty laugh and kissed my navel. My cock came up like a periscope investigating the action.

Ron Jaworski looked grim when the Eagles lined up after the kickoff return. The shadow of Super-bowl XV hung over him and he probably couldn't help having visceral memory flashes of his defeat at the hands of the Raiders. Nevertheless, he began mixing up his plays coolly and, just before the quarter ended, Philly was back on the board again to make it twenty to seventeen. Rushing through a hole made by Grinder Meade, linebacker Freck Foley leaped like a heavyset gazelle to block Tony Franklin's kick for the extra point.

Twenty-seventeen, Philly's favor, was where it stood going into the final quarter. My sighs at this state of affairs brought consolation from Stephanie. "Poor Steve." She kissed the very tip of my prick. "They'll come back." Her long fingernails furrowed the hair over my groin. "Don't you worry." Her long nipples brushed my thighs ticklingly as she bent over me.

But the Philly defense seemed grimly determined not to end up as the scapegoats they'd been the year before. Hairston and Harrison, the left and right ends, kept rolling off Nuke Outlaw and Plowboy Palmer to keep the kind of pressure on Terry that prevented her from setting up for the long pass. Short gains carried the Stonewalls well inside Eagles' territory, but then—disaster! The Philly outside linebacker, Jerry Robinson, intercepted a crucial pass and, with the clock starting to run out, the Eagles once again had possession.

"Damn!" I reacted.

"Now, now." Stephanie slipped to her knees beside the bed.

All I could see was the top sheen of her red hair between my thighs. But I felt her tongue as it dipped deep under my balls to lick the sensitive area there. "Ahhh!" Her facile tongue drew the exclamation of pleasure from me. Warm and wet, her lips formed around my right ball. Between my eyes and the TV screen my prick loomed up like a tower.

Whittier had that savage look defensive teams get in the last minutes of a game when their side is behind and they're operating on reserve energy. Behind their safety masks, their lips were curled like the fang-filled mouths of trapped cougars. Grinder Meade was coming on like a steamroller, knocking aside everything in his way to get to the ball carrier. Ambrose Pierce slid off the blockers like greased lightning on every play. Even though it was obvious that Philly was playing a running game and not chancing an interception, Foley and Sabbath, the Whittier linebackers, were playing bump-and-run so viciously that two possible Philly receivers were carried off the field.

This kind of desperate—but effective—defense held Philly so successfully that, in the end, they were forced to punt. Once again, Whittier had possession of the ball, this time on their own twenty-seven yard line. There were three minutes left to play in the game.

"Now!" I breathed a fervent prayer. "Let's go now!" I addressed the close-up of Terry Niemath on the TV screen as she called an audible at the scrimmage line.

I'm not sure if Stephanie misunderstood or not. In any case, she drew my prick deep inside her warm, wet mouth and licked the sensitive head voraciously. One of her hands squeezed my balls as she did this. The other one was between her own legs, toying lightly with her exposed and quivering clitoris. By angling my head, I could just barely see her fingers playing in her pussy as she sucked my cock. It distracted me from the game.

248

Abruptly she stopped, removed her mouth from my stiff prick and looked up at me. Her red lips were glistening, her green eyes sultry, her breath coming in quick, erotic little gasps. "I don't want you to miss the game," she said. "You keep watching. Don't pay any attention to me. I'll just keep on doing what I like to do. But you watch your Superbowl." And once again her sensitive and innovative mouth enveloped me.

I watched the screen. The Eagles' defense was set up to guard against the expected passing blitz. Terry frustrated them with a series of hand-offs and fakes for the kind of short yardage that nevertheless added up. Thus, as Stephanie drew my cock deep into her throat so she could lick my balls while sucking it, the Stonewalls made their way to mid-field.

The two-minute warning sounded. . . . Stephanie withdrew her mouth to rest a moment and squeezed my straining prick between the soft, panting globes of her firm white breasts . . . Terry handed off to her running back for five yards . . . Stephanie rubbed one of her long, red nipples into the widestretched hole at the head of my cock . . . Terry completed a sideline pass to Pete Gorgonzola, who stepped out of bounds with one minute thirty-seven to play . . . Stephanie stood up alongside the bed to pull off her nightgown. The black silk slid up her voluptuous body with a rustle, the sensuality of which was confirmed by her straining nipples and honey-coated pussy-lips and by my hard-bucking cock . . . Two more of Terry's passes went incomplete and the clock continued to run . . .

Stephanie stretched luxuriously, her tall, beautifully proportioned body shimmering in the flickering light cast by the TV screen ... Terry's third bullet in a row connected and she had eked out another first down with fifty-seven seconds left in the quarter ... Stephanie stretched out beside me carefully, not blocking the screen, and rubbed her hot, damp cunt against my thigh ... Forty-two seconds left and six yards short of another first down ... "I'm so hot!" Stephanie murmured in my ear. "You can keep watching the game, but please—Please!—fuck me now!" ... Third down, one yard to go and thirty-six, thirty-five, thirty-four seconds left in the game ... "I'm going to straddle you so you can see," Stephanie promised, suiting the action to the word. Crouching with one knee on either side of my hips, she slowly—savoringly—lowered her raw and quivering pink pussy over my upstanding cock until it pressed down and spread out over my groin. "Oh, God!" Her breasts swayed wildly back and forth as she rocked to increase the sensation of my hard prick filling her clutching quim ... Twenty-three seconds left, and Terry called Whittier's last time-out in order to go over to the sidelines and confer with Coach Newtrokni. She came back in with Horseshoe Cohen. They were going for the field goal ... "Fuck me!" Stephanie's sharp fingernails clawed underneath me as she moved up and down along the length of my prick. I felt her clitty rubbing hard with the movement and the way she moaned testified to the arousal of the contact. "Fuck me!" she repeated and I began to thrust upward, deep and hard, in tempo with her movements ... The kick was good! The score was all tied up at twenty-twenty with eight seconds left in the final quarter ... Stephanie stretched her long legs out full-length up my body so that my hard-pumping cock might penetrate her more deeply. I grabbed her hips and pulled her to me as I continued to move in and out of her clutching quim. The inside of her pussy felt like an oven around the frankfurter of my lust ... my balls bouncing against the underside of her thrusting ass, the two of us fucked away those last eight seconds of vain endeavor for the Eagles and sudden death overtime was now the situation facing both Superbowl teams ... "Harder!" Stephanie panted as the beer commercial preceding the sudden death period came on the screen. "Faster!" She ground down on me so that her cunt circled my cock in such a way as to stimulate every tactile surface of both organs. "Oh! You fuck so goo-oo-ood!" Stephanie groaned. "Don't stop! I'm coming! Soon! ... Soon! ... Soon I'm going to come!" ... The team captains faced off. The referee tossed the coin to see who was going to receive. It spun high in the air ... "FUCK! FUCK!" Stephanie scrambled to change position. She flung herself on her back and doubled her body so that her long legs locked around my neck. She pulled me over on top of her. I stabbed my frothing cock into her gaping, hungry cunt and resumed screwing her like a jack-hammer. "YES! YES!" Stephanie's arms flailed wildly behind her. "FUCK! FUCK!" ... As the coin fell to the ground, her hand tangled in the wire to the TV set, pulling the plug. The screen went dead. . . . "NOW!" Stephanie bleated "I'M COM-ING! I'M COMING! I'M COMING! . . ."

Stephanie came!

I came!

Can anybody tell me who won Superbowl XVI?

* * *

* * *

WORLD WAR II
FROM THE GERMAN POINT OF VIEW

SEA WOLF #1: STEEL SHARK   (755, $2.25)
by Bruno Krauss
The first in a gripping new WWII series about the U-boat war wag-
ed in the bitter depths of the world's oceans! Hitler's crack sub-
marine, the U-42, stalks a British destroyer in a mission that earns
ruthless, ambitious Baldur Wolz the title of "Sea Wolf"!

SEA WOLF #2: SHARK NORTH   (782, $2.25)
by Bruno Krauss
The Fuhrer himself orders Baldur Wolz to land a civilian on the
deserted coast of Norway. It is winter, 1940, when the U-boat
prowls along a fjord in a mission that could be destroyed with each
passing moment!

SEA WOLF #3: SHARK PACK   (817, $2.25)
by Bruno Krauss
Britain is the next target for the Third Reich, and Baldur Wolz is
determined to claim that victory! The killing season opens and the
Sea Wolf vows to gain more sinkings than any other sub in the
Nazi navy . . .

SEA WOLF #4. SHARK HUNT   (833, $2.25)
by Bruno Krauss
A deadly accident leaves Baldur Wolz adrift in the Atlantic, and
the Sea Wolf faces the greatest challenge of his life—and maybe
the last!

*Available wherever paperbacks are sold, or order direct from the
Publisher. Send cover price plus 50¢ per copy for mailing and
handling to Zebra Books, 475 Park Avenue South, New York,
N.Y. 10016. DO NOT SEND CASH.*

THE DYNAMIC NEW WARHUNTER SERIES

THE WARHUNTER #1: KILLER'S COUNCIL   (729-5, $1.95)
by Scott Siegel
Warfield Hunter and the Farrel gang shoot out their bloody feud
in the little town of Kimble, where War Hunter saves the sheriff's
life. Soon enough, he learns it was a set-up—and he has to take on
a whole town singlehandedly!

THE WARHUNTER #2: GUNMEN'S GRAVEYARD
(743-0, $1.95)
by Scott Siegel
When War Hunter escapes from the Comanches, he's stuck with
a souvenir—a poisoned arrow in his side. The parched, feverish
man lying in the dust is grateful when he sees two men riding his
way—until he discovers he's at the mercy of the same bandits who
once robbed him and left him for dead!

THE WARHUNTER #3:
THE GREAT SALT LAKE MASSACRE   (785-6, $2.25)
by Scott Siegel
War Hunter knew he was asking for trouble when he let lovely
Ella Phillips travel with him. It wasn't long in coming, and when
Hunter took off, there was one corpse behind him. Little did he
know he was headed straight for a rampaging band of hotheaded
Utes!

*Available wherever paperbacks are sold, or order direct from the
Publisher. Send cover price plus 50¢ per copy for mailing and
handling to Zebra Books, 475 Park Avenue South, New York,
N.Y. 10016. DO NOT SEND CASH.*

ADVENTURES OF A SOLDER OF FORTUNE:

THEY CALL ME THE MERCENARY #1:   (678, $2.25)
THE KILLER GENESIS

Hank Frost, the one-eyed mercenary captain, wages a war of vengeance against a blood-crazy renegade commander!

THEY CALL ME THE MERCENARY #2:   (719, $2.25)
THE SLAUGHTER RUN

Assassination in the Swiss Alps . . . terrorism in the steaming Central American jungle . . . treachery in Washington . . . and Hank Frost right in the middle!

THEY CALL ME THE MERCENARY #3:   (753, $2.25)
FOURTH REICH DEATH SQUAD

Frost must follow the bloody trail of sadistic neo-Nazi kidnappers, himself pursued by a beautiful agent who claims to be their victim's daughter!

THEY CALL ME THE MERCENARY #4:   (809, $2.25)
THE OPIUM HUNTER

Frost penetrates the Siamese jungle in a campaign against vicious drug warlords—and finds himself up to his eyepatch in trouble!

THEY CALL ME THE MERCENARY #5:   (829, $2.50)
CANADIAN KILLING GROUND

Protecting a seven-year-old genius turns out much harder for Frost than he thought. He gets trapped between the Mounties and the PLO, and there's no way out!

ADVENTURE FOR TODAYS MAN

SOLDIER FOR HIRE #1: ZULU BLOOD   (777, $2.50)
by Robert Skimin
Killing is what J.C. Stonewall is paid for, and he'll go anywhere and kill anybody if the price is right. In Zimbabwe, he must infiltrate the inaccessible mountain camp of a fierce warrior chieftain, and gets caught in the middle of a bloody revolution. Stonewall's instinct for survival is as deep as the jungle itself; and he must kill . . . or be killed!

SOLDIER FOR HIRE #2: TROJAN IN IRAN   (793, $2.50)
by Robert Skimin
Stonewall loathes Communists and terrorists, so he is particularly eager for his next assignment—in Iran! He joins forces with the anti-Ayatollah Kurds, and will stop at nothing to blow apart the Iranian government!

THE SURVIVALIST #1: TOTAL WAR   (768, $2.25)
by Jerry Ahern
The first in the shocking series that follows the unrelenting search for ex-CIA covert operations officer John Thomas Rourke to locate his missing family—after the button is pressed, the missiles launched and the multimegaton bombs unleashed . . .

THE SURVIVALIST #2: THE NIGHTMARE BEGINS
                                         (810, $2.50)
by Jerry Ahern
The United States is just a memory, and WWIII makes the 1940s look like playstuff. While ex-CIA covert operations officer John Thomas Rourke searches for his missing family, he must hide from Soviet occupation forces. Is Rourke the cat or the mouse in this deadly game?